Dreams About Food

Dreams About Food

A Collection of Short Stories and Poetry

Ben Ingram

Dreams About Food, a nonprofit organization
Oxford, MS

DREAMS
ABOUT
FOOD

First Edition, November 2018
Cover Illustration by Chance Flint
Copyright © Dreams About Food, LLC
1739 University Avenue Suite 195
Oxford, MS 38655

ISBN-13: 978-0-578-41728-8

All proceeds of this book go towards the Benson Reed Ingram Scholarship Fund at the University of Mississippi Foundation. To donate, visit dreamsaboutfood.com.

Printed in the United States of America.

To Ben's dog and true love, Charlotte.

"A story told by the conscious mind has a beginning, a development, and an end, but the same is not true of a dream. Its dimensions in time and space are quite different."

— C.G. Jung

Table of Contents

Why Ben Thinks We Should Read

If you ask most students around here if they want to read a book, they will probably respond with, "Hell naw, I ain't readin' no gosh darn book!" Getting kids to read a book can be a real challenge because today's students hardly ever want to read. They complain and moan every time a teacher assigns a book. Their new age brains have been tempered to more fast paced forms of media such as television, movies, and videogames. These new activities occupy every corner of their brains, leaving no space for tedium like reading which is left huddling in the streets trying to stay relevant.

Books can hardly compete with such formidable foes. When kids are looking to get a quick fix of entertainment, television or videogames are always there. Books, however, offer much more than most T.V. shows, movies, and videogames combined. Nothing stirs the imagination as books do, they allow the reader to create worlds and characters and exotic places and creatures all in the readers mind. One does not even have to leave his or her room to go on wild adventures or visit the future. If students find an appreciation for books early, they will be lovers of reading for life.

— Ben Ingram

Argument essay for Ben's freshman writing class at the University of Mississippi, courtesy of Tyler Ricketts

In Language Only a Twin Can Understand

A little over a year ago, my twin brother Ben hanged himself. Mom called me hysterically with the news. *Lee—Ben's dead. Get home.* In a panic, I stuffed a week's worth of clothes in a grocery bag and hopped into the passenger seat of my girlfriend's car. As I sat down, my ass burned but I hardly noticed. It was July 22, 2017, and a vicious Oxford, Mississippi sun had been tanning the car's leather seats.

My girlfriend drove the car, since there was no way I could have driven myself. My panicked hands shook so violently I looked as if I had developed Parkinson's. Surely, I would have jerked the steering wheel and flipped her car into a ditch. *Wouldn't that be great,* I thought. *I'm on the way home to see my dead twin brother and then I die, too.* At the same time, the idea of dying didn't seem so bad.

Blurred images of trees swept by the road's shoulder as the car barreled south on I-55 toward home. I fidgeted in my seat and readjusted the seatbelt under my arm to get more comfortable. Anxiety radiated throughout my whole body, and spikes of anger and depression took turns occupying the black pit forming in my stomach. Feeling hopeless, I focused on my breathing and tried my best to accept what was happening.

I rolled down the passenger window. The July heat raged, and the air outside smelled of hot asphalt. Helplessly, I watched the sky and prayed for a message from Ben telling me he was okay—wherever he was.

No response.

The blue sky was ethereal with beams of light piercing through puffy white clouds. *Wow. Maybe I've just never paid this much attention,* I thought. *But the sky sure looks beautif—*

"Don't be a dumbass, Lee." Ben interjected. "People always say some stupid shit about the sky when someone dies. If you take a picture of it today, I will fucking kill you."

Umm…Ben? That's not the message I had in mind.

The monotonous two-hour drive to Madison dragged on, my thoughts of Ben accelerating with every passing second. I needed a distraction, so I plugged the aux cord into my phone and turned on the Beatles album, *Revolver.* I skipped to the last song "Tomorrow Never Knows."

Raaaa-aaa-aaa-shaa-waaaaaa-shaawa. The droning of George Harrison's Indian sitar roared and sent a shock down my spine, while Ringo Starr's cracking snare and thundering tom-toms joined in suddenly, like bombs dropping. Meanwhile, Paul McCartney's hypnotic bass guitar followed with a steady groove. For the first verse, John Lennon chanted soothing, contemplative lyrics. *Damn. Ben loved the shit out of this song.* My mind floated downstream into another realm, releasing my pain and leaving an empty void behind. I closed my eyes and imagined Ben dancing and singing along.

Next came Ben's favorite part: Lennon's chaotic electric guitar solo. The solo had been recorded in the studio normally then played back in reverse before being put on the album, creating a psychedelic sound like an FM radio cutting in and out. The notes struck me like lightning bolts as each consecutive riff answered the previous one, as if by some strange, shamanic language. The energy of "Tomorrow Never Knows" became so intense, it felt like my soul was being airlifted out of my body. As I kept my eyes closed, an image of Ben's face appeared in my mind's eye. He looked like an angel, smiling back at me. *Damn,* I realized. *It was Ben who first introduced me to this song. Oh god.*

My eyes welled as my pent-up emotions surged upward, and I cried. Vivid memories of Ben and me together in his car jamming "Tomorrow Never Knows" at max volume flooded my head. Weeks-old bags of Whataburger and half-empty water bottles flying all over his car as Ben, with one hand, took screeching high-speed turns that left you holding on for dear life. Simultaneously, he'd bang his other hand on the dashboard to the beat of the music like a tribal warrior. He banged like this so often there was a spot on his dashboard rubbed raw.

To add to the mayhem, Ben would keep his car's stereo turned up LOUD. And, if you complained, without fail, he'd turn the volume up LOUDER saying sarcastically, "Is this better?"

Riding shotgun with Ben was like traveling through a wormhole—dangerous but pure euphoria. You could only hope you emerged the same person on the other side.

Awkward beginnings... Awkward beginnings...Awkward beginnings... Awkward beginnings... Awkward beginnings... Awkward beginning... Awkward beginning

"Tomorrow Never Knows" faded out with Lennon's final chant, and the world shimmered itself back into its harsh reality. *Shit. I wish this song was longer than three minutes.* My musical commune with Ben was short-lived and now just another fleeting memory. As my awareness gradually returned, a stinging thought arose in my head.

Ben and I can never listen to music together again.

The car approached the house where Ben took his last breath. I opened the door to get out and I planted my feet on the driveway. A setting sun casted an orange twilight across the yard while a cool breeze rustled the tree leaves above. My limbs moved haphazardly, as if I were on pain medication. The people standing outside the house looked inanimate, like *Monopoly* pieces, all facing me. No one spoke or moved. They just gazed at me with sorrowful, dark eyes.

"Where is my family?" I asked.

A bony finger pointed toward the house. My stomach sank as I paced toward the front door. *Fuck. I can't believe this is happening.* I placed my hand on the curved handle and pushed the latch with my thumb. The door wasn't a quarter open before Ben's dog, Charlotte, stormed in my direction and licked me. She smiled from ear to ear and her tail wagged like a helicopter. *She doesn't understand yet.*

I crossed over the threshold and through the foyer, stepping over Ben's shoes he carelessly left on the floor. I entered the living room, swiveled to my right and froze. Ben's bedroom stood just fifteen feet away. A spike of adrenaline shot into my veins. My throat tightened, and my vision tunneled. My chest felt like it was being pulled into the room by some supernatural force. *Don't go in there. Just close your eyes, turn around and go back to the car. You don't have to see him like this.* The pulling intensified and my knees shook like I was in an earthquake. I braced myself on a nearby armoire, and I edged along the wall. Ten feet away. A sharp ringing formed in my ears like the static from an old television. Immediately upon my recognizing it, the sound disappeared. *There is something strangely familiar about that ringing.* The hair on my neck stood up as I inched closer to the bedroom. Five feet away now. *Rzzzngggggggggg.* The ringing returned with increased intensity, like a dentist's drill. *Agh! What is going on?* My eyes fixated on a Miles Davis poster on Ben's wall.

Suddenly, a draft of cold wind blew over my face. Charlotte's ears perked up as she growled and charged in my direction. The barking became distant as my soul lifted upward. *Rzzznggggnnnzzzggggggg.* Everything around me faded into a black emptiness. *Ben? I'm scared. Are you there?* Finally, in a flash of orange light, the ringing reverberated throughout the universe with cleansing clarity—speaking a language only a twin can understand.

Ben? I'm so glad to talk to you. I'm here and I'm listening for real this time. Dude, I'm not even mad right now. I'm just scared and hope you're okay. God, just stop that shit. You were never good at apologizing. It's all good. I forgive you. I know things had gotten tough. Must be nice taking the easy way out. Chill out. It's just a joke. This is all so fucked up. I know you sent me your note last year—I know you told me your plan ahead of time—I know you didn't want anyone to hurt. Everyone just thought you were doing so much better. I really thought you were improving. You played us all like a fiddle, obviously. Stop laughing, asshole. You're one sinister motherfucker, you know that? I won't let you die in vain. I promise. No, Charlotte doesn't know yet. Okay. Talk soon. I love you.

Rewind to a few years before Ben committed suicide. We were both studying at the University of Mississippi ("Ole Miss"), home to one of Ben's favorite writers, William Faulkner. Ben was double-majoring in English and Philosophy with an emphasis on Creative Writing. I took the safer route and chose to study accounting. I envied Ben for getting to take intellectually-stimulating courses like Philosophy of Mind or Post-Modern Literature. On the other hand, my Income Tax class was so mind-numbingly dull I became paranoid it was speeding up the process of balding. *Perfect,* I thought. *I'll have one of the highest paying degrees but also no hair.*

When it came to Ben's lifestyle in college, I'd never seen anyone gain weight faster. He could have written the book on how to make straight A's doing nothing but eating Taco Bell, playing video games and drinking beer. He lived in pure filth, and he loved it. However, as much as Ben cherished a slovenly lifestyle, he needed to make a change. During his junior year, he decided to apply to the Ole Miss honor's college as a late entrant. This was Ben's first real step to challenge himself, as getting in was no easy task. Hundreds of juniors at Ole Miss apply each year but only fifty are allowed in. Ben courageously went for it anyway.

I remember hearing from Ben when he found out he was accepted. Ben's well-deserved achievement gave him a boost in spirit that you could see on his face. He was absolutely thrilled and, in an instant, his entire life changed for the better. However, in twin-brotherly fashion, Ben would occasionally use his newfound success to fuck with me.

"Hey, Lee," he said.

"What's up, Ben?"

"I'm in the honor's college now."

"Congratulations. I forgot from the last time you told me."

"You know what this makes me, right?"

"What?"

He smirked. "The smarter twin, noob."

"You do realize you're getting a liberal arts degree, right? What are you going to do with that?"

"At least I'm not going to be some miserable bean-counter corporate slave like you, bitch."

"Thanks, Ben."

"Just face it, Lee, he said. I'll *always* be the smarter twin."

"I really don't care."

"Yeah. Riiight. Which twin was born first?"

"Does one minute really make a fucking difference?"

"I don't know, does it?" (It did.)

"Jesus. Why are you so obsessed with who was born first, Ben?"

He chuckled. "That sounds like what someone who was born second would say."

"Fuck off."

"You know, being born first means my brain is more developed than yours."

"Bullshit. You know, Mom had a C-section. Don't you think we came out at the same time?"

"Read the birth certificates, fuckface. I was born at 1:46, you were 1:47. Na-na na-na boo-boo, I was born before you."

"Well, what if Mom didn't have a C-section and we were born naturally? Who would have been first then?"

"Quit speculating, Lee! Are you really going to argue with something as legally sacred as a birth certificate? Facts are facts!"

"Did you seriously just say, *legally sacred?*"

"Is there anything more sacred than law?" he asked. "Say double-entry accounting and I will fucking murder you."

"Fine. But in another universe, I think I would have been born first."

"I was born first in literally every possible universe."

"Really now?"

"Yes, really." Ben said, with finality. "On September 24th, 1993 at 1:46am all the stars and planets across the universe aligned in perfect union while I, Bensonite, was brought into the world precisely fifty-seven seconds before you—my inferior, parasitic counterpart."

"What? Who is this Bensonite person?"

"Your C-section theory holds no merit. Mom's OB/GYN specifically chose to pull me out first. Not you. Your big ass head was probably in his way and frightened him. He chose the more desirable twin."

"Funny."

"Also, get this. Did you know that the Board of Obstetricians recently decided that OBGYN stands for Omniscient Ben Governs You, Noob?'"

I grinned. "Shit. That's pretty good."

"You don't have to tell me. I already know."

"Just accept the damn compliment."

Ben shook his head. "I don't want to give you the satisfaction."

I conceded. "Okay. You win. Wanna go eat Whataburger?"

"Is that even a question? Abso-fucking-lutely. But, one more thing."

I sighed. "What now?"

"I'm in the honor's college and you're not, dumb fuck."

As much as he enjoyed throwing it in my face, Ben took being in the honor's college very seriously. His grades were stellar, and his professors and classmates loved him.

"Ben spoke up regularly, always being the first one to answer my hardest questions," said Leigh Anne Duck, one of Ben's English professors. "Ben loved learning and was truly generous and kind to those around him."

Unlike most honor's students, Ben went against the grain of boring research projects and chose to pursue a creative path instead. He decided he would write a collection of fictional short stories which he titled *Dreams About Food*. Ben's willingness to go all-in on a creative thesis ended up paying dividends, as he was able to attract the interest of Ole Miss creative writing professor and published author, Tom Franklin. Ben approached him about becoming his thesis advisor to his short stories, and Tom accepted.

"Ben was a natural storyteller. He loved short stories and fiction," said Tom. "I admired his writing. It was as funny as he was. Ben was a true class clown in the best way possible." Tom's stamp of approval for his potential as a writer gave Ben an additional boost of confidence that he wore proudly.

Ben toiled for almost a year crafting the stories in *Dreams About Food*. When he finally let me read them, he was so nervous that he had to leave the room. I was the first person aside from a few friends and professors with whom he had ever shared the stories, as he didn't think he had anything worthy of being shared. Boy, he was wrong.

Ben ran down the stairs and poked his head into the living room.
"Have you started reading yet? What do you think?" Ben asked.
"Ben. I'm barely through the first paragraph. Give me a minute."
"Alright sorry. I'm just fucking nervous, okay?"
I sighed. "Dude, I'm sure they're good."
"Just promise you won't lie if you don't like them. Give it to me straight. I can handle it."
"I will. I promise. Now, let me read! I've been waiting for months!"
"Can't wait to let you down, Lee," Ben joked as he darted back up the stairs.
I grinned with excitement as I read a few sentences. Ben's written voice sucked me in instantly. I couldn't put the paper down. *Holy shit. This is fucking good.* As if by some involuntary impulse, I began laughing hysterically like an Elmo doll. Ben's footsteps thumped as he raced back down the stairs.
"See, I knew you wouldn't like them. Give me my stories back."
"Are you serious? Fuck no! I'm still reading!"

"Huh?"

"Quit being so damn insecure, Ben. I'm laughing because your stories are hilarious! They're freaking brilliant!"

Ben's eyes lit up from my compliment. "Oh. Really? Don't fucking lie to me."

"Just go back upstairs so I can keep reading."

Lee Ingram
November 11th, 2018
Oxford, Mississippi

To donate to the Benson Reed Ingram Scholarship at the University of Mississippi, visit DreamsAboutFood.com.

Part One

Stories and Poetry

by Ben Ingram

By a Conjunction of Planets

Then Ben wailed again, hopeless and prolonged. It was nothing. Just sound. It might have been all time and injustice and sorrow become vocal for an instant by a conjunction of planets.
- Faulkner, *The Sound and the Fury*

A pile of half-empty bottles of water with brittle labels loosely hanging on and crushed cans of Coca-Cola and Red Bull bounces off the passenger floor mat as he drives over a pothole. The water sloshes around. His mother always says the sound makes her seasick and begs him to clean it up, but whatever, it doesn't bother him. He usually lets the pile accumulate until trash spills out when someone opens the door. Some people, when sitting shotgun, hover their feet over the pile so as not to touch it. He wonders what this says about them. Others just stomp it with their shoes.

Woods of neatly plotted trees surround both sides of the parkway. A film of hazy cloud obscures the sun. He checks the time on his phone: 12:34, shit he's late. He plugs an aux cord into his phone and plays "Chameleon" by Herbie Hancock, turns the volume just high enough not to rattle the speakers and cans, then picks up a vaporizer from the cup holder and brings it to his mouth. *Concentrate.* He pulls hard with his lungs, holds the smoke at the tip of his diaphragm, cracks open the window and releases a dense fog that gets sucked outside. A bitter wind whips around his face; he rolls the window back up. Easy now, hands on ten and two as he approaches an intersection. No other car there. He stops. A tingling sensation wash over him. He feels lighter. He concentrates his gaze over the steering wheel, his vision now choppy, as if projected onto a screen at a rate lower than twenty-four frames. Hands and feet numb, he drives on.

From the right a bird smacks into the windshield. He curses, screeches to a stop, the pile of trash rattling. He sees it through his side view mirror, seizing in the median. It looks like a chickadee, but he can't really tell. Goddamn suicidal birds, no chance in hell for it. In England, they call chickadees tits. He had read that on Wikipedia. Once, when he was ten, he shot a chickadee with a cheap plastic pump-action pellet gun. With him was his friend Parker who had big buck teeth and bushy brown hair. They were in an empty lot at the end of their street that backed up to the woods. Poised behind a mound of dirt, he took aim at the bird on its perch and fired. It fell on the dirt and flopped around with its wing, stirring dust into the air. They walked over and knelt beside it. He reached his hand toward the bird and it pecked his finger, causing it to bleed. He wanted to help it, but Parker convinced him that it was too late, took the gun, pumped it with air and pointed it at the bird's head. He shot, splitting it open. Its brains looked yellower than he expected. It looked like a cracked egg. They dug a hole with sticks in the ground and buried it, pounding the dirt on top. That was a long time ago.

The music stops. His phone rattles in the cup holder. He picks it up and pulls out the aux cord. It's his mother. "Hello. Yes, I'm pulling in now. I don't know, Caesar I guess. Bye." He sets his phone down and turns left into a high end outdoor mall named *The Renaissance*, perhaps because the city is under the impression that they've reached a cultural high point. Past the outskirts of the mall is an Italian restaurant called Colombo's. He pulls into the parking lot, turns off the engine and steps out the car. It's bitter cold outside; he's only wearing a flannel and jeans. He pushes through the door into the waiting room with dark leather benches along the walls, in the shape of a **V**. Cool jazz came down from the speakers in the ceiling, maybe Miles Davis? A hostess, wearing a white collared dress shirt, stood at the podium, smiling. "How many?"

"I'm meeting my family." He looks to the left into the bar, spotting them in a booth tucked in the corner. "I see them now." He walks over. Facing him is his younger sister Hannah. Opposite are his mother and his grandmother whom they call Meemaw. Besides the bartender, they're the only people in the room. The sun casts beams through the window, illuminating the motes of dust over the cream colored tablecloth. Outside a paper birch sways in the wind. He places his hand on his

4

grandmother's shoulder. She turns to look at him. She's wearing a beige turtle neck sweater and a mink coat. She places her bony hand on his, her arm adorned with gold bracelets.

"Well hi, Andrew!" Her voice is high and nasally, almost like she had inhaled helium. "How are you?"

"I'm doing good, Meemaw. How about yourself?"

"Good! I'm doing just fine." She has a smile on her gaunt, sagging face.

"You're late," says Hannah. She's wearing jeans and a navy sweater.

"Oh gee, I am? I'm terribly sorry. Mind scooting over?"

She slides out of the booth. "You can sit on the inside."

"But I don't like the inside."

"Sucks." She looks at him cryptically, as if to ask *Are you high?*

"Fine." He slides in and she after. "But what if I have to go to the bathroom?"

"Then I'll get up."

He looks at his mother. She's wearing a greenish gold turtleneck sweater. "High Mom."

"Hello Andrew," her voice raspy.

"Where's Dad?"

"He had to meet a client."

"That's too bad."

The three of them look very much alike. Slender, with thin noses, brown eyes, and straight brown hair, except for Meemaw's, who has grey. They would have all been the same height if Meemaw hadn't shrunk considerably. Their uncanny resemblance has always been a matter of discussion among friends and family. In their house on a wall hang three framed pictures, one of his grandmother, his mother, and his sister, in a row, each taken for high school graduation. They look like time hopping triplets.

"I have some exciting news," says his mother.

"What?"

"Your sister got into grad school!"

"Oh, that's wonderful!" says Meemaw.

He turns to Hannah. "Congratulations."

"Wow, so enthusiastic."

"What school?"

"University of Washington."

"My goodness," says Meemaw. "That's so far away, practically across the country!"

"I know," says his mother. "I'm going to miss my girl. I wish she wouldn't leave us."

"Cry about it," he says.

"But God has a plan. She even got scholarships."

"You are just so smart," says Meemaw. "What are you going to study all the way over there?"

"Astrophysics."

"Huh?"

"Speak up," says his mother. "She can't hear you."

"Astrophysics," a little louder.

"Oh. I don't think they taught that when I was in school."

They laughed.

"You should host the next reboot of *Cosmos*," says Andrew. "That'd be the perfect progression. First a white man, then a black man, then a white woman."

"Oh yeah? Just like the presidency?"

"Yeah we'll see about that."

"Anyway," says his mother. "It's a great school. They say it's a Public Ivy."

"A Public Ivy?" says Andrew. "That's just a marketing ploy."

"Thanks, bro."

"I'm not saying it's a bad school. It's a good school, no doubt. I'm just saying that 'Public-Ivy' is a buzzword, like 'super-food' or something."

"He loves to outsmart everyone," says his mother. "That's why I think he should become a doctor. But an ethical doctor, not like Phil Blanton."

"Do you always have to bring him up?" says Hannah.

"He makes me sick."

"We know," says Andrew. "You remind us all the time."

"I just can't help it."

He yawns: the music makes him sleepy. "Has the waiter come for drinks?"

"He did," says his mother. "We got you a glass of water, right here, and a Caesar salad, but you can get a drink if you want. Just ask the waiter. He's taking forever though."

"I don't know, should I?"

"Maybe you shouldn't."

"You know what, I think I will."

The waiter walks up with three empty wine glasses and a bottle of chardonnay. He's bald and has tattoos covering his arms and crawling up his neck. He says his name is Josh. He's wearing a white collared shirt and black slacks. He struggles uncorking the wine. Once he's opened it, he pours a little into the mother's glass. She drinks it and nods. He pours the rest in the glasses.

"Sorry for the wait," he says. "I'll have your salads shortly."

"That's okay," the mother says, insincerely. "Don't forget the extra dressing."

"I'm not sure I want a salad," says Meemaw.

"You need to eat something Momma."

"Alright."

"I think I'll have a beer," says Andrew.

"What would you like?"

"I'll have a Sierra Nevada."

"Okay. I'll have it all out shortly." Josh walks away.

"Hipster beer," says Hannah.

"What? It's not even that obscure."

"I don't like this waiter," says his mother. "He's so slow."

"Huh?"

"The waiter's so slow," she says in Meemaw's ear.

"Oh."

"Give him a break," says Andrew. "It might be the kitchen's fault. You wouldn't know; you've never worked in a restaurant."

"So what."

"Y'all chill out," says Hannah. "He's probably doing the best he can."

"He's probably an idiot," says his mother.

"I mean you could be right," says Andrew. "We can't just rule it out."

"And his tattoos make him look trashy."

"I don't know," says Andrew. "I think they look pretty gangster."

"I swear, if you ever get a tattoo."

"I am. I'm getting my face tattooed on my ass."

"Don't be sarcastic."

"I wish I was."

"I am not in the mood."

"Sheesh, I'm just messing. I would never get a tattoo."

"Why not?" asks Hannah.

"I don't know, I guess I've always figured that whatever I think is cool in one moment, I think is lame in the next. So I would never be able to decide what to indelibly stain into my untainted flesh. My body's like a temple, right?"

"Wow, so deep."

"Yeah I know. The self's, like, an illusion, man. And attachment to material things corrupts the soul. Besides, most people's tattoos are so stupid and cliché."

"Aren't you judgmental? Maybe they're just trying to express themselves."

"What is one expressing with a Pokémon tattoo?"

"Innocence, maybe?"

"You see innocence, I see regression into a childlike state."

He's staring at the shelves behind the bar, at the different bottles of liquor, wondering which is the most expensive when the waiter returns with their salads and his beer. He places them on the table, says "Enjoy," then starts walking away when his mother says, "Excuse me, you forgot the extra dressing."

"I'm so sorry ma'am. I'll grab that now." He walks away.

"I told you," his mother says.

"Eh? Maybe your right," says Andrew.

"You should listen to your momma more often."

"Sure thing," he says. He stabs some salad with his fork and eats. It's a little dry. It needs more dressing. He takes a sip of his beer.

"How's the hipster beer?" asks Hannah.

"It's hoppy, with a hint of shut the fuck up."

"Dammit Andrew. Do you have to use that language in a public place."

"Chill out. We're the only people here."

"What was that?"

"Don't worry about it Momma."

"Talk about judgmental. Just let me drink my beer in peace."

"Cry about it."

"Haha, very funny."

"You eat like a pig."

"Prove it."

"When was the last time you ate McDonalds?"

"Yesterday."

"Point proven."

"Whatever. You with your kale and quinoa bowls. I don't have to submit to your fascist health standards. You think you're too good for McDonalds? That's pure bourgeoisie elitism."

"You really do eat like a pig, Andrew," says his mother.

"Yeah I know."

"Are you still going to medical school, Andrew?" asks Meemaw.

"I don't know. I'm still thinking about it. In the meantime I've just been waiting tables at the drive-in."

"Do you like it there?"

"You know what, it's not too bad. It keeps me busy, and the tip money's good. I got plenty to pay my rent and plus some to have fun. I also like the people I work with a lot. They're really cool."

"That's good."

The waiter walks back with the dressing. "Here you are," he says. "Again I apologize."

"That's okay," his mother says, smiling. "Thank you."

He leaves.

"Idiot."

They take turns pouring dressing over their salads. He takes another bite. It tastes better now.

"I know I've probably asked this a thousand times," says Meemaw, "But how long has it been since you graduated?"

"Three years," says his mother. "He'll be twenty-five next month. I still think he should go to medical school."

"I just don't think I want to. It's so expensive and takes years to get your license, and besides, most doctors are arrogant, miserable people. Why would I want to put myself through that?"

"Okay, how about this: Either you go to medical school, or you stay here, get married and have babies."

"Those are my only options?"

"Yep."

"Alright, I guess I choose that one."

"Which one?"

9

"The one you just mentioned."

"Stop fooling around. I mean do you really want to wait tables for the rest of your life? Just go to medical school. We need an ethical doctor in the family, unlike Phil Blanton."

"Why do you always have to bring up that damn doctor? Let it go."

"He makes me sick." She drinks her chardonnay.

"Can we change the subject?" asks Hannah.

He forks salad into his mouth. "Yes, but you know she will just bring it up again," mouth full of lettuce.

"Are you dating anyone?" asks Meemaw.

"I was seeing this girl for a while, but I broke it off."

"I liked her," says his mother. "I wish you didn't end it."

"Eh, I wasn't feeling it. Besides, I still get the occasional Tinder hookup."

"That's so shallow."

"Yeah, I know. It's awesome."

"What's that?" asks Meemaw.

"It's something on the Iphone, Momma."

"Never mind then, don't bother explaining it. I wouldn't have a clue."

The song changes, a trumpet plays its rapid melody. Sunlight falls onto the tablecloth, giving it a warm glow. While he eats his salad he sees another chickadee lands on a branch off the paper birch. At least he assumes it's a different one. Perhaps the first one is back from the dead. The chickadee tweets while they look at their menus.

"Momma, you've hardly touched your salad."

"I'm just not very hungry."

"Is the medicine working?"

"What medicine?" asks Andrew.

Hannah turns to him. "They have her taking Marinol."

"Marinol?"

"Mississippi just legalized it."

"That's hilarious." He turns toward Meemaw. "Can you feel it, Meemaw?"

"Yes. I just take the pill and I feel so happy."

They laugh.

"That's awesome," says Andrew. "I think we could all use some Marinol."

"I'm sure you use plenty," says his mother. "Eat more salad, Momma.

That medicine's expensive."

"I know a guy."

"Don't need to know that." She turns to her mother. "Do you want another glass of wine?"

"I think I do. By the way, who's taking me home after this?"

"Andrew said he would."

Meemaw turns to Andrew. "Oh, I hate for you to have to do that."

"I don't mind at all."

"Don't let me forget," says his mother. "I have a bottle of wine in my car that I need to give you before you leave. Hide it in her purse so the nurses don't see it."

"I can't believe how strict they are over there."

"Well, you can't really blame them. They're just looking out for her health."

"Yeah, but she's an adult. She should have the right to a bottle of wine."

"Huh?" says Meemaw.

The bird still sits on the branch outside, turning its head this way and that way mechanically. The waiter walks over to take their orders. He orders spaghetti with meat sauce and another beer. Meemaw used to make good spaghetti. She hasn't cooked in years. Hannah orders the shrimp cannelloni, his mother the lobster fettuccini with extra sauce, and Meemaw the smoked chicken ravioli. Josh takes their menus and assures them that he will have their order up shortly.

"Can you put this salad in a to-go box, please," says the mother, pointing to Meemaw's salad.

"Certainly." He takes their salad plates and walks away.

"You can eat that salad later, Momma."

"I doubt I will."

"Just try to."

Hannah turns to Andrew. "Why'd you get the spaghetti?"

"I don't know. Why not?"

"It's just kind of boring, don't you think?"

"You're boring."

"Thanks, bro."

"Move over; I got to use the bathroom."

"Thanks for informing me." She slides out of the booth and he follows. He walks around the bar and into the dining room, which is dimmer than the bar, the only light being the candles that flicker over the round tabletops. Waiters carry round trays holding either steaming entrees or empty plates. The room has its own gravitation. The roar of blended voices bounces off the walls. It reminds him of the beginning of *Sgt. Peppers*. In the hallway leading to the bathrooms hangs a payphone from the wall. He doubts anyone still uses it.

As the bathroom door shuts closed it snips off the sound from the dining room. He can only hear the jazz. It's just the drum and bass holding on to a steady, perpetual groove. The bathroom smells like lavender soap. He steps in front of the urinal, unzips his pants and starts taking a piss. As he stands his head starts swimming. When he's done he washes his hands and splashes cold water onto his face, dabbing it dry with a paper towel. There are four mirrors, in the front and back, and to the left and right. Is this what it's like to be stretched around the world in each cardinal direction?

The surge of voices returns as he pushes through the door. To his surprise the payphone is ringing. What the hell? He picks it up and places it to his ear.

"Hello?"

"Congratulations! You've won a free trip to the Bahamas."

He slams the phone onto the receiver.

The food has arrived by the time he comes back. He feels a certain satisfaction for this having happened. Hannah slides out to let him in. Steam rises from the spaghetti. It smells good. He sticks his fork into the middle and spins it around. He takes a bite. It's good, but not as good as Meemaw's. He looks out the window. The bird was gone.

Hannah has been trying to explain the process of planetary accretion to Meemaw.

"Save your breath, honey. This is way over my head."

12

"That's not what the bible says happens," says his mother.

"There's a lot the bible doesn't mention," says Andrew. "For instance, Mary was artificially inseminated by aliens."

"My gosh," says Meemaw. "Is that so?"

"Yes, Meemaw. Listen to the Marinol. Let it guide you towards the truth."

Meemaw's eyes widen. "I think I get it."

"Momma please ignore him. Andrew, are you taking your meds?"

"Fuck the meds. They are a poison."

"Listen to the doctor and take the damn pills. You're not the only one.

I don't know why you make such a big deal about it."

"I don't trust the pharmaceutical companies."

"I bet you don't trust the government either," says Hannah.

"You know who else I don't trust?"

"Who?"

"This waiter. I think he's giving me the eye."

"You should be flattered."

"It's weird. It makes me uncomfortable." He takes a big gulp of beer. "I know I look good. I don't need this dude to ogle me. I feel objectified."

"I think this is some sort of narcissistic delusion."

"Dammit. Don't psychologize on me. That's not cool."

"You do that shit all the time."

"Cause I'm good at it. Stick to your planetary play sets or whatever nerd shit you do."

"You're just mad cause you know I'm right."

"What difference does it make? It's like all relative, man. And technically, you're both alive and dead right now, so it sucks to be you."

"But you're observing me alive right now."

"Okay, so if I just close my eyes, and with all my strength imagine you dead…"

"Stop it!"

"What? Are you afraid it will work?"

"Unconscious murder wish!"

"Damn, you're right. My Bad." He eats some spaghetti and takes a sip of his beer. He feels better having food in his stomach.

13

"Well Hannah," says Meemaw. "You'll have to visit often."

"She's right," says his mother. "We're really going to miss you."

"I couldn't agree more," says Andrew, taking a swig of beer. "We are all going to be just destitute without your graceful presence."

"Do you always have to be such an ass?" asks his mother.

"Don't worry Mom," says Hannah. "You still have the babies."

"You and your dogs."

"They don't talk back to me." She looks at Meemaw. "Momma, you haven't even touched your food."

"I'm just not hungry."

"Please take at least one bite.

Meemaw picks up her fork and knife. Her hands tremble as she cuts off a corner of ravioli and lifts it to her mouth. She chews slowly and swallows.

"Is it good?"

Meemaw nods her head slowly.

"Eat as much as you can."

Andrew finishes off his spaghetti and takes a long swig of beer. The horns take turns soliloquizing to each other. He feels much better being full. "If she's not hungry don't make her eat. She can take it home and eat it later."

His mother glares at him. She mouths *she needs to eat.* "Take another bite, Momma," she says.

"In a minute."

"I want to watch you eat it."

"Please Lucille. Just give me a moment."

"Just one bite."

"For Christ's sake," says Andrew. "Give her a break."

His mother's face furiously flushing, "Don't take the Lord's name in vain!"

"My bad."

"And don't be sarcastic with me!"

"Will y'all please just calm the f down," says Hannah. "The bartender probably thinks we're insane."

"This family is insane," says Andrew.

"Well can we at least act like sane for one meal? I swear sometimes I think I'm the only one in this family who has a fucking grip."

14

Andrew finishes off his beer. "So happy for you sis. Thanks for keeping a lid on our dysfunctional family. What would we do without you, our shining star?" He belches.

"Dammit Andrew!" says his mother. "You know I don't do burps."

"That's strange. I happen to love burping." He burps again.

"I can't believe you would be this rude in a nice restaurant!"

"I think I need to go to the ladies' room," says Meemaw.

"I'll walk you there," says Hannah, embarrassed. She slides out of the booth and stands next to Meemaw with her elbow extended. Meemaw wraps her arms around Hannah's elbow and together, with their combined strength. Meemaw gets out of the booth and steadies her feet on the floor.

"You okay, Meemaw?" asks Hannah.

Meemaw smiles. "I'm doing just fine." Arm in arm, they walk into the dining room.

Andrew and his mother glare at each other. She sips her wine. The waiter walks up and asks, "Can I interest y'all in a dessert?"

His mother goes blank.

Andrew stares Josh in the eyes. "We'll pass," he says. "In fact, why don't you make yourself useful and bring us the check."

"Uh...Yes sir. I'll be right back." He walks away.

"He really is slow, isn't he?"

She says nothing for a while, takes a sip of her wine. "You don't have the right to tell me how to treat my mother. If I say she needs to eat, she needs to eat. I'm trying to see that she makes it to Christmas because this could be her last. One bad fall and she's gone."

"You've said that the past five years. Think about it. Five years worrying, all that time, wasted. And you know it's coming regardless. It could be tomorrow, it could be five more years. There's no point in guessing when it will happen only to have her exceed each estimation. Until, of course, the day it actually happens. You're trapping yourself in a constant cycle of worry which is driving you crazy. Which is driving me fucking crazy."

She drinks the rest of her wine. "You know, maybe you shouldn't go to medical school. You're vicious; you just have to pick on somebody, and why's it always have to be me? Who's to say you wouldn't be as vicious as Phil Blanton."

"Please. You can't compare me to him. That's not fair. And you know what? It's not my fault you gave him the perfect opportunity to take action. You've put this whole family in jeopardy."

"Meredith is my best friend! Do you have any feeling in that cold heart of yours? She said that asshole surgeon of hers masturbated in front of her! All while she was under anesthesia! And then when she rightfully presses malpractice charges he tells the court she's fabricating her story because she's on meds that distorted her memory. It's just not fair the way they treated her! I mean lots of people take meds! You take meds!"

"I haven't taken any medication for three months, and I'm doing just fine, don't you think?"

"Is that why you've been such an asshole? I bet you don't even believe Meredith's story."

"See, that's where you're wrong. I do believe her. And generally, I believe he's as much of an asshole as you say he is. And that's where I think you fucked up. You were so obsessed for justice that you forgot how vicious he is. I mean this is the type of man who would stop at nothing to gain advantage for himself. Did you think he would just ignore what you spread about him? Think about it, he's a prominent plastic surgeon that works on women's tits for a living. All the housewives in town go to him, he wasn't going to let this get out of hand. He had to set the record straight, his record, that is. Again, I don't deny her story; I believe her, I really do, but what you did was you made serious accusations about him. Criminal accusations. You gave him no choice but to bounce back, and let me tell you what I think is going to happen: you're going to lose. I wish it wasn't like that but you won't be able to prove shit in court. That's just the way it is. You know what he did to her, what made you think he wouldn't do the same to you? Or worse? And there's nothing any of us can do. I don't know why you figured justice would prevail. This isn't fucking HLN; it's more like a Lifetime movie."

"Do you think this is funny? Do you even care about this family at all?"

"Sure, I do. In fact, I'll tell you what; I'll give you an ultimatum. Either I enter into Medical school, say Johns Hopkins or maybe Princeton, yes Princeton. They say it's numero uno. So, I enter Princeton Medical School, speed through every class in like one month, passing with flying colors and they're all like holy shit this man's a prodigy. I speak at the commencement address. They award me the highest honors, put me in the revered Hall of Fame, my legacy sealed for all time. Then, I start my own plastic surgery clinic to face off against the Evil Phil Blanton. With the almighty power of strong narcotics, silicone, and the Bible I force a confession from his cursed lips, winning you your Nancy Grace justice porn headline and saving the day.

"Or, and I want you to really listen to this one, because I think it's good. I feel much more prepared and comfortable with this one. Pretty please pick option B. Being, as you are, obsessed with revenge against Phil Blanton, I assume you know where he lives. I bet you even drive by sometimes. Anyway, you tell me his address and I'll tell you what I'm going to do. I'm going to drive by his house and make sure nobody's home. I'll go sometime after lunch, while the kids are still in school and he's at work. I'm guessing he lives in a rich neighborhood, so he probably sets his alarm at night. The afternoon's my best opportunity. I'll park my truck somewhere close by but not too close so to be inconspicuous. Between my chair and the console is an old rusty hammer. I keep it there in case I ever get robbed. I'll step out of the car and slyly place the hammer into my pants, just under my shirt. I'll walk around to his backyard to see a doggy-door in his back door. I'll hop the fence. A dog will creep out of his doghouse, but he's old, doesn't see too well, barely recognizes that I'm there. I'll squeeze through the doggy-door.

"Once I'm inside, I'll have to decide where to hide. I'll come out around midnight, so I'll need to consider the most unlikely place they would enter. I'll think, of course, the attic. I'll find it through the closet in the master bedroom upstairs, enter and wait. I'll sit Indian style, back straight, mentally preparing myself for hours. The heater's on; the attic's sweltering. Sweat will roll down my forehead, soaking the collar of my shirt. I'll sit there for ten hours straight. By midnight I'll be ready, I'll be purified. I'll take off my shoes, tie the laces together and hang them around my neck. I don't want anyone to hear me. As slowly as I can I'll twist the doorknob and step into his closet. I'll peak through the crack in the doors, see him sound asleep on the right side of his bed, facing up. gingerly step to the side of his bed. At this moment I'll have to decide: blunt end or pointy? And where? Pointy end right through the frontal lobe. That'll do the trick. Then, very quietly, I'll walk out the front door, and toss the hammer somewhere safe where no one will find it. Down the sewer? No, they might check there. Perhaps at the bottom of a lake. I'll work out the details later. I'll have plenty of time to think it through while I'm waiting in the attic. I think this is the surest way to justice. It's much more pragmatic than option A."

His mother just stares at him for a moment, looking a little concerned. Eventually she says, "Do you want people to think you're fucked up, or do you just not care anymore?"

"I don't know, maybe I don't. Everybody's always saying you should care all about this and that. You should care about the trees, the breeze, the seas; the birds, the turds, the fucking words you use. And I think, what good does it do? Does it really make a difference? Is it even worth the effort?"

"You have no faith."

"Not in this world."

"You need a woman in your life."

"Sometimes I can barely stand the women already in my life."

"You can't blame me for all your problems."

"I'm not."

"So, what then? Do you want to wait tables for the rest of your life? Is that what you want? To be a loser?"

"We're all losers. The Phil Blantons of the world won a long time ago."

"Maybe you're right. Either way, I don't really want to talk about it anymore. In fact, why don't you go wait in your truck? I think Meemaw's ready to leave."

"Whatever." He slides out of the booth and stands up.

"Get in a better mood. Get back on the pills."

He grins wide, says "Sure thing!" and walks away.

As he's leaving the hostess smiles and says, "Have a nice day!"

"Thanks! You too!"

He exits the restaurant and steps into his truck, closing the door behind him. He pulls from the vaporizer. "Goddammit Andrew. Why'd you have to say all that?" He looks down at the pile of trash. "Shit," he says, tossing trash into the backseat.

Hypnagogia

I was sitting in English class thinking of escape routes in the case of a terrorist attack. This felt more urgent than the discussion of our summer reading. It seems like every week another incident pops up on the news. How can I be so sure that it won't happen here? The truth, of course, is I can't. You got to prepare for all possibilities. In terms of probability, there's got to be at least one motherfucker in this school that has made a list of all the people he wants to kill, like that greasy kid that sits in the back of class drawing pictures of samurai or ninjas or some other shit. He seems like a pull the wings of a fly kind of guy. You know what, that's not fair, I've done that too. But I felt kind of bad afterwards. I just wanted to see if they'd be walks. They were; I kept them in a jar and fed them sugar water. I went on walks with my walks and we watched *The Walking Dead* together.

That was a lie. I'm sorry.

Where were we? My mind tends to wander. Right, English class. It was the first block of the first day of school, a Wednesday, and my mind was still groggy. Outside was dark and overcast. It looked like rain was coming. Mrs. Wilcheck and the class discussed *Brave New World*. I didn't read it, but I read the sparknotes. I wasn't going to read a book assigned to me. That takes out all the fun. And this was assigned over my summer break. Besides, it's too tempting to just look up a summary on the internet. Although, this book did seem pretty interesting. Kevin, the guy sitting to my right, mentioned something about "orgy porgy gives release." I'm not sure what that means, but I must admit; I'm intrigued. Suddenly, the thought came to me: What if a terrorist with an AK-47 blasted down the door and barged in. I happen to sit closest to the door, so I'd have to act, if for no other reason than he'd probably shoot me first. What would I do? I know no form of martial arts. I could try to jab a pencil in his neck, but the lead would probably break. So I decided to knee him right in the nuts. Under normal circumstances, I would never hit somebody in the nuts, on principle. But this was the exception. Charlie Wyman's theorem: You may kick someone in the balls if and only if (*If Fuh Fuh*) that person is a terrorist.

That's the thing about balls: they're weak. I learned all about the reproductive system last year in Human A&P. We even watched a live birth. The woman had this big black bush, and all this green goo squeezed out with the baby. I didn't know babies popped out so quickly like that. Of course, I wouldn't know; I was born by C-section. That's why I don't get why some men say women are the weaker sex. Are you crazy? They're tough as shit. If you told a man that he has to carry a person in his stomach for nine months, then push that person out of his body through a small hole, and that afterword that person would give you titty twisters with its teeth for up to two years, that man would say, "GET THIS THING THE FUCK OUTTA ME!" Abortion would be legal everywhere. That pregnancy shit takes ovaries. And consider the relationship between the person and his or her respective organs. Ovaries come fully loaded, straight from birth. Balls start out all shriveled up like two little peas in a pod.

Ovaries: I'm gonna make you bleed, and when I'm through with you, I'm gonna make you think it's hot all the time.

Balls: I'm really sensitive, so please be careful with me. Push me higher on the swing, Mommy. *Weeeeeee!*

Charlie's paradox: Balls are basically big pussies.

Anyway, I would knee the terrorist in the balls, wrestle his gun away from him, and shoot him in the face. I wouldn't normally be the hero, but like I said, I have no choice here. I would then have to decide which way to escape: to the left down the stairs towards the foyer and out the main entrance? or to the right down the hall, down the stairs, and out back through the library. The latter seemed like the better option: they would probably be guarding the main entrance, but might overlook the library. Having solved this puzzle, a sense of relief fell over me.

That's when it started. Just to the left of the center of my field of vision, a small orange dot, the size of a pea, appeared. This is not to say that it appeared out in front of me. It appeared in my perception, and it followed the motion of my eyes. Its edges were jagged and morphing in a swimming motion. The colors bled out through the center. It was like watching a soap bubble through light. Dizziness wrapped around me, and I felt a tension build in the middle of my forehead that pulsed through my fillings. Slowly, the dot grew bigger, wrapping around the entire left side of my vision. Zigzags bounced around the edges. My ears were ringing. Outside the window the wind thrashed around a plastic grocery bag. The buzz of the florescent lights seemed louder. I felt terribly thirsty and wanted to puke. And then the colors faded away.

That's when the headache began. It was the worst pounding headache I'd ever experienced, and I felt sure I was about to puke. I couldn't have focused on class if I wanted to. It hurt to keep my eyes open. It didn't take long to determine that I was unfit for school. But how could I leave? I couldn't call home sick on the first day of school; no one would believe me. Then it occurred to me that I had just planned a route. I raised my hand and asked to go to the restroom and Mrs. Wilcheck handed me the pass. I stepped outside and gingerly closed the door behind me. I could barely stand straight; my head was swimming. I looked left, right and then left again, checking for assistant principals roaming the halls with their walkie-talkies. All was clear. I proceeded down the right and stepped down the stairs. My only exit was through the library, but I was certain the librarian would be sitting at the counter. I didn't have a note, only the bathroom pass, which was useless, so I threw it away. Just keep it cool, I told myself, and she won't suspect nothing. I pushed through the door.

Mrs. Finnegan, the librarian, stared at me from behind the counter to the left. She had on a bright yellow blouse that, in my present state, seemed to give off a glare. "Hello Mr. Wyman," she said. How did she know my name? I never go to the fucking library. "Do you have a note?"

I walked towards the counter. She continued to stare me down. She had glasses that hung to the cliff of her nose. Is that some kind of universal librarian code of conduct? I placed my hands on the counter. "No," I said.

She crossed her fingers together. "Why not?"

"My teacher...she uh...forgot, I guess. I didn't even notice. Careless mistake."

"Who's your teacher?"

"Mrs. Wilcheck."

"She's got a good head on her shoulders. I find it hard to believe."

"Well, you know, she's good and all, but far from perfect. Wait. I mean. Everybody makes mistakes, right?"

She let a ruthlessly awkward moment of silence pass. "I'll tell you what. You wait right here, and I'll go right into my office and give her a call. Don't worry; we'll clear this right up." She stood up and walked into her office, leaving the door open. I heard her take the phone off the receiver and punch the buttons. She leaned back and peered at me from the threshold. I flashed an awkward smile. As soon as she left the doorway I heard her say, "Hello. Mrs. Wilcheck?"

I booked it. As I walk walking through the door, I thought I heard my name called. I glanced back. There was a group of people, probably freshman (at least no one I knew) sitting at a table. They all stared at me looking puzzled. My mind must have been fucking with me. I pushed through the door. Although it looked like it was going to rain, the sun happened to be right between the clouds, beaming at me with all its brilliance. The intensity dazed me. I shut my eyes, but it had burned an impression that subsided for several seconds. I felt something crawl up my throat and then bolted over, heaving. It took several dry heaves before anything came up. The vomit came out my nose and dribbled down my mouth. Spattered against the pavement, it looked like a spicy brown mustard milkshake. I turned around to check if anyone had come after me. Up above the door was a white camera, pointing right at me. Shit. I hobbled down the parking lot, leaning forward, arms dangling, gasping for air. I came to my car, a black 2001 Jeep Cherokee, unlocked the door, and slung myself in the seat. I checked my face in the rear view mirror. Bile hung from my nostrils and the corners of my mouth, and red dots circled around my eyes. I had popped blood vessels from straining too hard. I wiped my face on my shirt and started the engine.

Luckily my neighborhood was right next to my high school. I took a right onto the parkway. I drove slowly, desperately trying not to stir my stomach. I blasted the AC. On the radio played nothing; I couldn't tolerate sound. I turned right at the sign that said *Welcome to Citrus Lake.* I stopped at the gate. It seemed to pulse, which nauseated me. I rolled down the window to punch in the code: 5555. The outside wind pumped into my car, rustling loose receipts, stray hairs and dust around my car. Perhaps it was the change in air pressure that caused my headache. I rolled up my window as fast as I could while the gate began its sluggish motion. Funny story: The week they installed the gates, my friend, with his brand new car, barreled through it, leaving a massive dent. He had dropped his phone, and while bending over to pick it up, failed to notice the gates defiance. Luckily, they never caught him.

Unfortunately, my house is at the very end of the neighborhood, past the lake. I rolled past all the stop signs, and in my stupor, failed to observe the speed bump, launching my skull into the ceiling. I swerved into the median and plowed into one of the new maple saplings they had recently planted. I think I lost consciousness for about five seconds. I really hate those fucking speed bumps. They're another one of the Neighborhood's latest projects. These are no ordinary, yellow speed bumps. These are obnoxious mounds built of red brick to match the fucking houses. They're so bad, my mother, who drives a Nissan Maxima, bottoms out every time she goes over them. I swear to God the assholes who ordered the installation of these things deserve beheadings.

See I have this theory on speed bumps. It goes like this: Speed bumps have an *explicit function* and an *implicit function*. The explicit function is to slow down the dutiful, observant driver, drawing his attention to his speed and surroundings in order to protect the innocent children whom we all love so dearly. The implicit function is to trick the absent minded, reckless driver like me (You know, I never understood the phrase *reckless driver*. It would seem to me that that would be a good thing) into thinking he just ran over one of those children. You're just driving along, not a care in the world, when suddenly you find the top of your head unfortunately close to the roof of your car. Before your mind has time to catch up and assess the situation, in that split second of despair before reason kicks in, you're thinking: Oh my God, I just killed someone, my life is over; I gotta skip town, scrounge my savings, swap identities. I'll never see my family and friends again. An eternity of fear is crammed into that little moment and you solemnly swear to God that you will never disregard the road again until you realize: God Dammit! They got me! Which brings me to the *subconscious function*: to remind you that they're fucking you in the ass.

When I pulled into the driveway the garage door was down. Hopefully no one was home. I sat in my car with the engine running, mulling it over. I must have dozed off for a second when I heard the check gauges light beep on. Something smelt like sulfur. Steam was pouring out the hood of my car when I heard a loud *pop!* , a thick fog forming over my car. Shit, I think my pipes busted. I don't know shit about cars, so I figured I'd just ask my dad about it later and forget about it for now. I turned off the engine and stepped out of the car. I punched in the code: 7777. Why were all these codes so stupid? The garage door slowly lifted in a loud clamor that reverberated through my head. Thankfully, no one was home. I closed the garage door behind me. Behind the back door the dogs barked and clawed. I pushed them away as I opened the door. They immediately took to jumping at my legs. "Get down," I said, shoving them with my knee. Luckily, they weren't big dogs. There was Zoe, a black Yorkshire terrier-poodle mix, or *Yorkie-Poo;* and Daisy, a white golden retriever-poodle mix, or, as my mom calls it, a miniature teddy bear golden doodle; which, in my opinion, is way too many fucking words. I mean which is it? A bear? A poodle named Teddy? I don't know; it's stupid. And is the word miniature necessary? Doesn't teddy bear imply that already? I mean Jesus Christ people! From now all dog breeds have a two word maximum, end of session.

The TV was playing in the kitchen. I think we have at least nine TV's in our house. Probably too many. My mom leaves the TV on for the pets when she leaves the house. She thinks it comforts them or something moronic like that. I keep telling her, they don't give a shit about the TV; but whatever. I'm not paying the bill; what do I care? Actually, come to think of it, my friend Mark has a pit bull named Sage who loves TV and will watch it with the most intense concentration, sometimes even jumping up on the counter to get closer. It's awesome. I wish my dogs did that.

My cat was sitting in a box atop the marble island, next to the sink. His name's Mr. Krinkle. He's an orange tabby with white splotches. He's old; his skin sags, exposing his brittle bones. He's on a special diet for his kidneys, and every morning my dad crams a couple pills down his mouth. He's got the bite marks to show for it. Lately, Mr. Krinkle has taken to wailing, usually in the early morning. I can hear it from my room upstairs, especially if the door's open. I give him six months, tops. I stroke him a couple times, then turn on the sink just slightly so it leaks out in a clear stream. Mr. Krinkle likes to drink from the sink. This reminded me how terribly thirsty I was. I grabbed a cup from the cabinet and filled it with ice and water. I had just taken a sip when I heard something. For the second time, I swear I heard my name being called. I thought, surely my heads just messing with me again. I mean, it's a pretty common phenomenon for people to hear their name being called when it's not. A sort of glitch hardwired into our brains. Yet this time I was certain I heard it. It was coming from the TV.

The channel was tuned to CBS. They were reviewing the results of a recent *Jeopardy!* tournament. And the winner was a guy named Charlie Wyman. He didn't look a damn thing like me, but we had the same name, spelled the same too. That's interesting, I thought. Staring at the TV, however, reminded how bad my head was hurting, and I felt my stomach squeeze. I opened the drawer to find some Advil, swallowed two pills, then drank down the rest of my water and turned off the TV. I went upstairs into my room, turned on the white noise machine, stripped off my clothes, turned the lights off and climbed into bed. I felt better being in the cool, dark room, though I was still wobbly. It was like when you go to the beach for a day, and then latter when you lie down to go to sleep that night, you still feel like you're floating. Eventually, I sank into a deep sleep.

I awoke deep in a thought. It was about hearing my name on the TV, but also all the events leading up to that moment. It all struck me as too coincidental. Now I know there are probably a million other jerk offs named Charlie Wyman saying, "Look honey! I'm on TV!" but that's not what's bothering me. It was the timing. I had walked in at just the right moment to hear it. If I came in just a minute earlier, or a minute later, I probably would have missed it. I definitely would have missed it if I never left school. I would have never left school that day if I didn't have that headache. And the TV just happened to be on that particular channel! I don't even watch *Jeopardy!* It's not the name itself that's bothering me; it's the conglomeration of all the coincidences. That's the thought I had: that somehow these events were all connected. It started vague, like looking at minnows through a murky creek, slipping in and out of perception. But eventually I was able to grasp ahold of it. It was also evident that the thought had started before I awoke, essentially before I was aware I was even thinking. Which also bothers me: Who's doing the thinking here? I guess I assumed that during sleep my thoughts were a sort of blank slate, but not anymore. Now, I'm not normally superstitious, but since these events had left this impression on me, I had to consider: If this is a sign or whatever, then what does it mean? Two things of a contradictory nature immediately popped out at me. On the one hand, it seems, I'm a winner, yay! On the other, I'm in jeopardy. Fuck. I scared myself looking too deeply at it. I figured this whole sequence started with another random, unprompted thought: that of a terrorist attack. That certainly fit in with this jeopardy theme. I could no longer find humor in such a situation. I thought, could this signify some future attack?

It was at this moment that I realized I had seriously overthought the whole thing. I mean terrorists, really? I'm sure everyone, on some level, fears being obliterated without a moment's notice. This is the post-Nuclear, post 9/11 era. It's a perfectly natural, normal response. And weird coincidences happen to people all the time; it doesn't mean they mean anything. Besides, it's dangerous to make connections that aren't there. That's how delusions unravel. I decided to put the matter to rest.

By the time I got out of bed, I realized I felt much better; sleep had worked its miracles. I checked the time on my phone; it was just past noon. I'd slept for about two hours. The throbbing headache was gone, but I still felt a little dizzy and foggy, and every time I coughed, a shock of pain went through my head, which was a problem, because I'm a chronic cougher. The best way I can describe how I felt is like the morning after a tequila bender. Not the worst, but not great either. So, I decided to do what I always do when I'm hung-over: smoke marijuana. I put on some sweat pants and a navy T-shirt, went into my bathroom, opened a drawer and took out a pill bottle, a white lighter, and a cigarette bat. I opened the bottle, pinched off a bit of bud, and carefully placed it at the end of the bat. I turned on the air vent and took the sploof out of the drawer. If you don't know what a sploof is, it's pretty simple. You take an empty roll of toilet paper, stuff it with dryer sheets, and put a sock over it. Of course, this is just the way I made it; there are others. You blow the smoke through the roll to absorb the stank. It works pretty well, I guess. Not that it really matters; my parents practically never come upstairs. I lit the end of the bat and pulled the smoke into my lungs, holding it for a few seconds until I blew it through the sploof. The coughing fit that came after was almost unbearable, but after a while I felt a lot better, or at least higher.

It wasn't long before I was struck with an intense, mind consuming hunger. I hadn't eaten all day. I hardly ever eat breakfast; I'd rather hit snooze five times, and today was no exception. Of course, I didn't eat when I got home; I probably would have chucked it up. But now that I felt better, and what with the weed and all, I could think of nothing else but food. Not just any food; I needed sugar. And then I knew exactly what I wanted: blueberry Toaster Strudel. I must have blueberry Toaster Strudel or nothing at all. Please God, let there be blueberry Toaster Strudel. I went downstairs into the kitchen and opened the freezer. In the shelf on the door was an unopened box of blueberry Toaster Strudels. Thank you Jesus; you've answered my prayers. Our God is an awesome God he reigns from heaven above with wisdom power and love our God is an awesome God. Our God is an awesome God. I popped the strudels into the toaster and sat down at the breakfast bar. To pass the time, I decided research my recent condition on my iPhone. I had to make sure I didn't suffer from an aneurysm, or a tumor, or a brain parasite. I have a somewhat obsessive fear of brain damage and brain ailments. Though, we're probably all a little brain damaged, right? It didn't take me long to discover I had suffered a migraine, with the added benefit of a preceding visual aura, which occur only twenty percent of the time, so lucky me. I had suspected this; I'm pretty sure migraines run in my family. Anyway, the internet assured me that this was not a life-threatening condition, so I could rest easy.

The strudels sprung up from the toaster. I got up, got out a paper plate and placed them on it. I squeezed icing in winding paths on top of the strudels. I must have still been a little wobbly, because when I grabbed the plate off the counter the strudels slid off onto the floor, one falling icing up on the floor, the other landing icing down onto my socked right foot. Normally if this happened I would throw them away and start over, but at this point I didn't really give a shit. I picked them up and gobbled them down. I even wiped the icing off my sock and ate that too. Afterwards, I was still hungry, so I put two more strudels in the toaster, and once they were done I gobbled them down. After that, I was still hungry, so I decided to eat two more. Having eaten the entire box, I finally felt satisfied, but this feeling was soon replaced by a sense of remorse. Did I really just eat an entire box of Toaster Strudel? I mean what the fuck is wrong with me? Do I have any restraint? This is a typical state of affairs for me. Excessive indulgence followed by shame and guilt. Just that constant struggle between my favorite comic book characters, the Id and the Super-Ego. The Id's like: you should jerk off, then binge eat pizza while you binge watch *The Wire*. Super-Ego: What the fuck is wrong with you? Do you have any dignity? You are not worthy of the life you've been given! Super-Ego's the real asshole; at least Id lets you have fun. You know, people say that Freud's theories are unscientific, and that they've been disproven, but whatever, I think they're funny; besides, what do people know anyway? Also, considering that there's a whole genre of porn dedicated to motherfucking, I'm starting to think he had a point.

To assuage the guilt I decided to take the dogs for a walk. I called the dogs from the kitchen but got no response. I walked into the den to find them asleep on the couch. They like to sit on top of the cushions, crushing them. "Get up!" I yelled. They craned their heads towards me. "We're going on a walk." That gained their interest. They jumped off the couch and scurried to the backdoor. I opened the door, took the leashes of the hooks, latched the leashes to the dogs and opened the garage door. The wind whipped through the cypress trees that lined the edge the driveway. We planted them there to block the view from our neighbor's garage, which happens to face ours. Up above dark clouds drifted across the sky. I'd better make this walk quick to not get caught in the rain. We set out, Zoe to my left, Daisy to my right. We started down the sidewalk and took a right at the corner before the cul-de-sac. Daisy suddenly stopped, causing me to jerk the leash. She was hunched over, taking a shit on the sidewalk. "Dammit Daisy, can't you go in the grass?" The shit was bright green and goopy. We strode off before anyone could notice. At the next corner, before I could take another right, Zoe stopped and lifted her hind leg to piss. Zoe's the type of dog that'll stop every ten yards to leave her mark. Luckily, she's a teeny dog, so if I keep a pace she has no choice but to walk as fast as her little legs let her. Again, we set out.

We reached the footpath that wraps around the lake. The wind was stirring the water. The circumference of the lake is about a mile. The lake was manmade to fit with the rest of the artificial ecosystem in which I dwell. I'm not sure why they call it Citrus Lake; probably because it's acidic from run-off. The lake drains into a concrete dam near where the main road meets the water. Empty Gatorade bottles and other trash often collect there. From here it flows under the street into a sloped waterfall made of cement and large rocks. The water runs into a pool with a drain in its center. Basketballs often get stuck in its vortex. I've always wondered if it's strong enough to suck down a person. Probably not.

About half way around the lake was a black man sitting on a white bucket at the edge of the water, casting a rod and reel. He was wearing a blue trucker hat and chewing on a toothpick. He had a scraggily goatee. "Catch anything?" I asked.

"Nothing man."

"That sucks. Probably the weather."

"Yeah. Yesterday I caught two brims and a bass."

"Nice." I looked to my right where the gym and pool was. It looked like it was closed. All the lights were off. To the right of the Gym is a field. In the center was a black dot of crows. It was like they were holding a council meeting. *On Thursday, we will shit over the BMW dealership. All in favor say aye.* I turned back towards the man. "Good luck, man."

"Appreciate it."

I walked on. To the right of the pool, above the woods and against the clouds flowed a steady stream of blackbirds. Their combined voices filled the air. I couldn't see where they came from, but they seemed to be endless. Through the woods is a winding path. I don't know why, maybe it was the birds, but I felt compelled to walk it. The wind was swaying the branches of the trees. Once I stepped into the woods the air around me darkened. Cigarette butts, broken beer bottles and crushed beer cans cluttered the forest floor, their labels faded by time. To the left of the path is a gully lined with smooth sandy mud where water sometimes flows. Our feet crunched the leaves beneath us, each with a distinct timbre and rhythm from the difference in our weight and steps. The sound of the blackbirds overhead grew to a roaring pitch. As I was walking down the path I was thinking: you know what, I've never seen a snake back here, when out of the corner of my eye I caught something curled up and squirming, causing me to jump forward, jerking the dogs with me, and let out a screech for which I became embarrassed afterwards. I looked back to see a speckled king snake. They say king snakes are good snakes because they eat other snakes; but doesn't that make them cannibals? Whatever, it was leaving me alone, so it can't be too bad. I continued walking. At the end of the path I came across the strangest sight. In the soft mud of the gully stood an old man, barefoot with his khakis rolled up to his knees. He had a thin tuft of white hair and liver spots that adorned his skull. He was just standing there, arms hanging from his side, staring into the middle-distance with an expression of pure befuddlement. I said "Sir, are you okay?" and he slowly turned his head towards me, opening and closing his mouth like a fish out of water. He could produce no sound. "Uh, well, you have a nice day." I turned around and walked back to the road.

When I got back the streets smelled like rain. Over the lake swirled a massive, billowing cloud, deep blue in color. Against the reflection in the in the water it looked like a bowl of ice cream with whipped cream. Dammit, why am I always thinking of food, now I'm hungry again. I picked up my pace. Thunder rumbled in the sky. Still the blackbirds carried on. How many could there possibly be?

As I turned the corner to my street rain began to fall in big gobs. I started running but by the time I got to the garage I was soaked. To make it worse, my mom's car was parked in the garage. I checked my phone for the time: 2:37; I'm not supposed to be home for another hour. I was stuck, my car broke down, and the rain was coming down hard. I unleashed the dogs, hung the leashes on the hooks, and walked through the door.

She was sitting at the breakfast bar, drinking a Diet Coke. She was watching the weather segment of the local news. When she saw me she put down her Coke and stared me down. "The school called. You've been suspended."

I rubbed the back of my neck. "Oh gee. That's too bad."

"On the first day of school! Really?"

"I was sick, I swear to God. I had a migraine. I even puked; look at my eyes, I popped the vessels."

"Ugh, I don't want to know about that. Why didn't you go to the office and call me?"

"On the first day of school? Who would believe me? Besides, I didn't want to look like a huge puss."

"Don't say that word. I hope you know you are not to leave the house for the duration."

"Doesn't matter anyway; my car broke down."

"What happened?"

"I think the pipes burst, but I don't know; I was going to ask Dad about it. How long am I suspended for?"

"Two days. You go back Monday."

"Nice, extra-long weekend."

"Charlie! This is not funny. Thanks for walking the dogs."

"Yeah no problem."

"They're saying on TV that the tropical storm in the gulf has increased to a class three hurricane, and shows no sign of stopping. School might get canceled."

"Lucky me. What's its name?"

"Leroy."

"Leroy? Have they run out of the good ones?"

"I guess so."

"Well, anyway, let me know if we need to take shelter."

With nothing to do, I turned on my Xbox and played *Call to Arms: Advanced Arab Fighter IV* for about five hours. I then realized how much time had passed. It's so easy to lose track of time while playing videogames. It hit me; I'd just spent five hours in a mindless violence simulation. I know it's not real, but started feeling bad for enjoying it. I mean what does this say about me? I was at my friend Kevin's house the other day. He was watching videos from the camera feed of an AC 130 gunship on YouTube. You could hear the airmen talking to each other, commanding fire on the targets bellow. Since the footage was in negative, the targets were white, anonymous silhouettes. I thought: this looks just like the videogame. I felt kind of sick.

So, I turned off the Xbox and settled for a more enlightened form of entertainment, television. I turned on my Apple TV and selected Netflix. I decided to watch *Mad Men*. It was only five minutes in when I started craving a cigarette. That's the problem with *Mad Men*: I can't watch it without wanting a shot of whiskey and a cigarette. I looked outside the window to see that it had stopped raining. Hopefully I could slip out without my parents noticing; they don't like me smoking. I grabbed my pack and went downstairs. I could hear the news playing in the den. I walked in to find both parents passed out on the recliners. They each had stemless glasses of red wine resting on their stomachs, just about tilting out of their hands. The sight was strange; usually one of them falls asleep while the other nags them to wake up. But they were both out cold, mouths open, snoring. Well, I figured, now they definitely won't notice me slipping out. Outside I could hear the cicadas singing their ethereal tone. Fog rose from the road into the dark clouds that covered the sky. I leaned against the trunk of my car and lit a cigarette. As the flame extinguished, I noticed something just below the clouds, in between my neighbors' houses across the street. Three orange lights in a triangle formation just hovering there. The sky seemed to bend around

31

it, like it was made of mirrors. It emitted a faint hum. I just stared at it. After about a minute it glided away to the east, barely producing a sound. I took a puff of my cigarette. I thought, why didn't I take a picture of it with my iPhone? It just didn't occur to me. In fact, it was like my mind went blank. I felt nothing. I finished my cigarette and went back inside. When I was in my room, I noticed how tired I was. I took off my clothes, turned off the lights and fell asleep in bed.

That night I had a strange sequence of dreams. I found myself in front of a bank with faux classic columns that my city favors so much, because they think they're a high point in civilization or something. Except wrapped around this bank were red and blue McDonald's PlayPlace tunnels. I stepped inside, the doors closing with a thud behind me. A bank teller in a burgundy uniform stood in front of a winding red velvet rope line.

"Applying for loans?" she asked.

"Uh, yeah, I guess."

"Excellent!" she said, extending her arm behind her. "Please wait patiently in line." There was no one in line. At the end was the entrance to two tunnels, a blue one on the left with a *Subsidized* sign and a red one to the right with an *Unsubsidized* sign. To the left was a measuring stick with a *You must be this tall for subsidized loans* sign. My head came just below it. I started up the red tunnel when I notice behind me, at the mouth of the tunnel, stood an anachronistic grimacing greaser wearing a black leather jacket and jeans, holding a switch blade. "I'm gonna cut your balls off and feed 'em to my dog!" he said, crawling in after me. I frantically squirmed my way up and down through the tunnel. At one point he grabbed my ankle, but I kicked him in the face with my other foot. "You're fucked now, motherfucker!" he said. I kept crawling until I came to the exit. I tumbled down into a ball pit with red and blue balls. The greaser laughed at me from the exit. "Looks like you're shit out of luck." The balls started swirling around me. My legs were being dragged from under. I struggled to stay at the top, but eventually I was exhausted and sucked down below.

The next thing I know I'm on a deserted beach at night. In front of me is a massive vortex of black clouds, thunder and lightning illuminated the waterspouts that lined the horizon. Behind me were three high-rise condos, their windows shattered, no lights were on. All across the beach were piles of trash and debris: smashed TVs, molded

32

couches, refrigerators, washers and dryers, microwaves, toaster ovens, trash cans, broken bottles, Styrofoam coolers, beach chairs and big umbrellas, damp newspapers, wet magazines, tables, desks, computers and computer chairs, lamps, paints, statues, pill bottles, syringes, wheelchairs, books, clothes, towels, and every other miscellaneous item. Above flew a red biplane with a sign trailing its tail that read: *EAT MOR CHIKIN.*

When I awoke I couldn't move. A sense of dread overwhelmed me. My eyes stayed shut. An electric shock sensation swelled through my forehead, sending shrills through my teeth. I felt what I can only describe as a presence move around my room. I felt for sure that if I looked something bad would happen. Then it stopped.

It's been storming all day. I've been pacing back and forth upstairs, replaying yesterday's events over and over in my head. I've come to two conclusions: either I'm going insane, and it was all an illusion, or what I saw was real, and something is watching me, perhaps even manipulating events around me. Both terrify me. If I'm going insane, well then that's that, but if what I saw was real, that just opens up a whole other set of questions. First off, what was that thing? And more importantly, what do they want with me? Are they good, bad? Probably, they don't really give a shit. Can they read my thoughts? Can they control my mind? And what the fuck, if anything, does Chick-fil-A have to do with this? This morning I noticed a strange indentation in my forehead that started at the top and curved down to my right eyebrow. I thought, has this always been there? Just some natural formation of my skull? Or did they open me up and pick at my brain? I can't be sure of anything anymore. Should I tell somebody? I don't think I can trust anyone with this; they'll surely think I'm crazy. No, best to keep this a secret. No sense in sharing it with anyone. I kept saying to myself just try not to think about it, it was just some random occurrence, it's over now and it doesn't mean anything. Though I couldn't help thinking, and maybe I'm self-pitying, but why does this have to happen to me? I'm not some *thing*; this is my life! Come back down here you assholes! I got some questions for y'all! Over and over and yet I can't make any sense out of this. My reels are spinning out of control.

That night I couldn't sleep, so I took two Benadryl, a melatonin tablet, and some valerian root capsules. I climbed into bed I tried focusing on my breath. After a while, a funny sensation came to me. I wasn't' quite asleep, I was still in my room, yet I felt as though I were floating on my back in the ocean. I heard a stream of chromatic piano tones. It made me feel strange, so I shook myself out of it, and tried to go back to sleep. But again I fell into the same state, except this time, I heard what sounded like a female voice speaking through an intercom, yet I couldn't make out the words. I checked the time, 1:23, got out of bed and went to the bathroom and switched on the lights. I turned on the facet and splashed cold water on my face. In the mirror my reflection looked grotesque, unreal. My eyelids sagged and my eyes seemed out of place, crooked. My hair was stitched on, my face claylike, mushy. An itch crawled down my back. I couldn't stand to look at myself.

I went downstairs to find my mom still awake. "Can't sleep?" she asked.

"No. What are you still doing awake?"

"I'm cleaning the kitchen." Piled in and around the sink were all sorts of dirty dishes. She hadn't gotten far. "It stopped raining," she said.

"Must be the quiet before the storm."

I went out back. In the woods behind my house the cicadas sounded. Above was a thin veil of clouds. The full moon hung in the sky, casting a brilliant aura through the clouds that created the impression of a hole. I stared at it.

My mom came outside and looked up with me. "Oh my goodness," she said, stunned. "It's a miracle!"

"Uh…yeah."

She smiled warmly. "God is good. We're going to be okay."

The Angel Taxi

Silence, healing.
  -Heraclitus, *Fragments*

He stands smoking a cigarette, staring through the glass of an art gallery at a painting of a wizard. A stereotypical wizard, with a blue hat and a matching robe, painted vibrantly, almost cartoonish. He has a long grey beard that hangs below his belt. Swirls of pink and yellow light above and around him. It's late, the bars just closed. The outside air is hot and sticky. His shirt clings to his skin. Wisps of fog surround the rooftops. It looks like it might rain, yet somehow, he feels that it won't, that the clouds will refrain. He turns toward the courthouse and starts walking, his left hand tucked into his pants pocket, clutching the lining.

A crowd of people beside the Blind Pig holler at a drunk girl wearing high heels. She flicks them off with both fists then turns around and moons them. The crowd cheers, and the girl stumbles and falls face-down on the sidewalk, some gentleman from the crowd rushing to help her up. A cop on horseback clops around the corner and starts asking questions. There's always something going on. He had had a few beers but he doesn't feel drunk. In fact, he feels more alert than usual, a peculiar tension in his solar plexus, like having a string in his stomach pulled taut, picking up the slightest motions around him. A streetlamp buzzes overhead. Something inside his mind wonders if it's because of him. The thought makes him sick. Who is he? He assumes no set answer. Still like a lamppost, his mind escapes him. At different junctures, different people. He tries to blend in, but he can never be sure that his insides are safe. Do his thoughts boil with the contents of his stomach? Is a four pronged personality poking through his shirt? He can't be sure of what feeds into his mind.

She was wearing red lipstick to match her dress. What was she saying? "Where've you been? I haven't seen you in a while." She has pale green eyes.

"I don't know. Around I guess." He was leaning his arm against the rail. Below the balcony flashed police lights. A cop was giving a man a field sobriety test. He didn't stand a chance.

"Hmm…That's not a sketchy answer or anything. Do you still go to the house?"

"No, I dropped."

"What? Why?"

"I guess I just lost interest."

"Just lost interest? What's up with you? You're acting all cagey."

"What do you mean?"

"See that's exactly what I'm talking about. Be upfront with me. Why did you really drop?"

"Well, like I said, I just lost interest. And I guess I started thinking the whole thing was kind of fucked up."

"Fucked up how?"

"Did you ever take Psych 201?"

"Yeah."

"Do you remember the Stanford prison experiment?"

"Oh please. You can't be serious."

"In a way, I am."

"There are a lot of good guys in that house."

"There are some really bad ones too. And sometimes I ask myself where I fall on the line."

"You're a good guy. I can tell."

"I don't know. Sometimes I think I'm the fucking devil."

"You think too much."

"You're probably right."

He sees a cab on North Lamar and waves at it. It's a champagne colored minivan, the company Angel Taxi. The driver rolls down the passenger window. He's bald with deep creases set in his forehead, the expression of a granite statue. "Need a ride?"

"Yeah, mind if I sit shotgun?"

"Sure, go ahead."

"Cool." He flicks his cigarette onto the sidewalk, opens the door and slides in the seat. A guy wearing a camel hair jacket over a navy collared shirt sits behind him, next to a blonde woman wearing a blue sun dress. The cab driver pulls around the courthouse onto South Lamar. "Where am I taking you?"

"Forty-two Aspen Loop."

"Alright, I'm gonna drop these people off first, then I'll take you there."

"Sounds good."

"I still can't believe we have to pay ten extra dollars," says the blonde. You can smell the booze on her breath.

"Y'all are outside city limits."

"By like two miles. Give us a break."

"Can't, company policy." He pulls into the chevron with the chicken on a stick. "I gotta get some gas." He parks next to the pump and steps outside to go pay at the register.

"It's fucking bullshit. These companies have a fucking monopoly on this town and set all these stupid rules."

"Look, I got it covered." said the guy. "You don't have to worry."

"Still, he could cut us some slack if he wanted to. Ugghh...whatever. He's a fucking nigger."

"Will you just relax?"

"Ugghh!" She crosses her arms. The cab driver walks out the station and to the car, unscrews the gas cap and puts in the pump. The passenger sits quietly in shotgun listening to the gas surge into the tank. He has nothing to say. He never does during a cab ride; he prefers to listen. Cab conversations are always interesting. Under the cover of darkness and drink people tend to transform into a baser self. The last time he rode in a cab there was this marine sitting up front with a pudgy female driver wearing a shirt that was a little too small, so that her sides bulged out of it. She talked of how she wanted to join the Army, how she had scored in the 98th percentile on the ASVAB, but when they asked why she wanted to join, she said, "I just want to kill people." Hmm, she's surely on some list, he thinks. You're not supposed to want to do that until after basic. There's an order of operations for these things. The marine, however, was charmed. He placed his hand on hers, which clutched the gearshift. "Can I be honest with you," he said. "I think I like you." It was almost endearing.

They pull out of the gas station onto University and turn at S 9ᵗʰ Street. "I wish I had bigger boobs," says the girl, unprompted. The passenger sneaks a glance. They look alright to him. The driver has to stop and wait for the people walking across the streets. Some of the pedestrians stumble as they walked, others shout at each other. Presently, they drive on. They are turning onto Jackson when two guys, a fat, dumpy looking one and slender one with a shrewd face and dark hair, both wearing black Vanderbilt game-day shirts and black, lizard-skin cowboy boots, walk into the street, holding up their hands. "I think these people need a ride," says the girl. The driver stops the car and rolls down the window. "I can take y'all home after these folks, if y'all need a ride."

"Sounds good," says the slender one, sliding open the door and stepping inside to the backseat, the fat one after him.

"Hi! I'm Mary Claire, this is Braxton."

"I'm Jeff," says the fat one.

"I'm Robby," says the other. "Nice to meet y'all." They all shake hands. The passenger watches them from the corner of his eye, but in the darkness can't quite make them out. He doesn't want to exchange information. They turn onto College Hill.

"Where're y'all from?" asks Robby.

"Jackson," says Braxton. "What about y'all?

"From Miami," says Jeff. "But we go to Vandy."

"Hell of a game," says Braxton.

"Yeah, well half of our line was injured," says Robby. "If we didn't have those turnovers we could have won. Mistakes were made."

"Too much football talk," says Mary Claire.

"What else would we talk about? It was a great game. You were there, you saw it."

"I've had enough of football for today. Let's talk about something else. So, what are y'all studying?"

"Risk management," says Jeff.

"I'm double majoring," said Robby, "psychology and economics."

"Cool!" said Mary Claire. "You must be really smart. What do you want to do with that?"

"Business Management. Learning the markets and the mind."

"Hey man," says Braxton. "You learn how to get inside peoples' heads and you can get them to do whatever you want."

38

"It's all it takes."

Don't let him inside your head. Oh no, here comes the noise again, entering through the back of his mind, faint at first but growing in intensity. The clamor of a bar at maximum capacity, a myriad maze of voices talking over voices. Individual voices fade in and out of perception as if governed by the Doppler Effect. He can't silence them; they have a will of their own. The string in his stomach tightens. *He's staring at the back of your head. Quick! Hide! He's watching you.* The passenger glances behind. In his periphery the faces meld with the darkness; their distinctiveness dissolves. *Shhh! They can hear us.*

They can't hear shit.

Robby's has ESP, telepathy. Don't ask me how I know this, I just know. I can tell.

I'm scared. He's watching us.

He's a CIA operative with a chip in his brain. He's running mind control experiments on unsuspecting students. He's the one drugging the water. I just know.

Crazy fucking loon. Ain't nobody drugging the water. Shit, he's the one getting inside their heads, listening in to their conversation like a fucking creep.

Shhh!

They turn into a neighborhood with cookie cutter houses, all identical except for the colors, and pull into one of the driveways. Over the doorway hangs a Confederate battle flag. "Alright, that'll be thirty dollars."

"Thirty dollars!" says Mary Claire. "That's fucking horseshit!"

This bitch complains a lot.

Yeah but I love her shoes.

"How many times do I have to tell you I got it covered," says Braxton.

Henpecked boyfriend

"I explained this when I picked y'all up," says the driver. "Ten per person, plus ten extra because y'all outside city limits. That's the rules, sorry."

"It's fucking exploitation, that's what it is," says Mary Claire.

With a sullen look, Braxton pulls out his wallet and hands the driver a twenty and a ten. "C'mon, let's go."

"It was so nice meeting y'all!" says Mary Claire. "I hope y'all enjoy Oxford. Have a good night!"

"The pleasure was ours," says Robby. "Hope to see y'all again."

"Likewise," says Mary Claire, flashing a big smile. Braxton, distraught, slides open the door and they step outside and walk toward the house, Mary Claire holding on to Braxton's arm, stumbling. They turn around to wave as the car drives away.

Oh no, now we're cornered.

"Nice people," says Robby. "So, where do you live?"

Don't invite him inside. He can't enter if you don't invite him inside.

You better lock your door 'cause I think this fag wants to fuck you.

"You're about to find out," says the passenger.

Good job genius. Now they think you're a fucking weirdo.

"Alright then," says Robby, slightly bemused. "Say, what's the deal with the bars closing so early around here?"

"That's just the way we do it in Oxford," says the driver. "Plus folks got church in the morning."

"Yeah, well in Miami the clubs stay open till five AM."

Fuck Miami. Miami's for fags.

"This ain't Miami," says the passenger.

"We maintain a certain order around here," says the driver.

"Yeah, whatever," says Robby. "Shit is weak compared to Miami. I bet you've never been to Miami."

He's baiting you. This is all part of a test. He's trying to elicit a response from you but don't let him. Just keep quiet.

"Sure haven't," says the passenger, crossing his arms.

"Aren't you the life of the party?"

Tell him to mind his own fucking business.

"Just tired, that's all."

"Tired? It's not even one o'clock."

That's past my bedtime.

"You're tired," asks Robby, "Wow. In Miami we…"

"Look man I don't give a fuck what y'all do in Miami."

You shouldn't have said that. That's exactly the kind of response he wanted.

Yeah you should be careful 'cause this dude could beat the living shit outta you.

Shit shit shit. Now they think you're fucking crazy.

"What the fucks your problem?" asks Robby, bulking up. "You know what? Fuck this town and all you dumb hicks in it. Hospitality my ass. You think you're something? You're not worth shit."

"Hey!" yells the driver. "That's enough! They'll be no fighting in my cab."

No fuck this guy! I know you got a pocketknife. Stick it in his fucking gut. That'll show him. You can't let this asshole talk shit like that. Teach him a fucking lesson.
He's a government agent! They'll lock him up for life!
He ain't shit. Fuck him.

They stay quiet for the length of College Hill, and then turn onto Anchorage, which is abysmally black from the lack of streetlights. "I don't like this," says Jeff, a slight tremor in his voice. "Can we turn on the radio or roll down the window or something?" The driver pushes the knob on the radio. It plays "Soak Up the Sun" by Sheryl Crow.
"That better?" asks the driver.
"I guess," says Jeff.
This song sucks.
I told you he can hear us. Shhh, be quiet!
Something skitters across the street. "Was that an armadillo?" asks the passenger.
"Sure was," says the driver.
Oh man I wish I had my gun.

They drive on, the headlights carving cones out of the darkness. He's almost home but the string in his stomach tightens more, the noise in his head grows louder. He can't concentrate.
"How much longer is this going to take?" says Jeff.
This dude's getting on my last fucking nerves shhh he can hear us don't invite him inside he can't enter if you don't invite him inside drugging the water quick hide, they think you're fucking crazy why can't you just act cool they can hear us shhh he's working for the government on mind control experiments you crazy fucking loon shhh! they're listening! What's he so freaked out for? Stab him in the neck and rip out his throat I'm tired of hearing him whine just do it!
The string snaps. The passenger jerks around and stares into the darkness of the cab. "Shut the fuck up! Shut the fuck up!"
Robby and Jeff stare, mouths agape. The cab driver turns toward him. "Hey! Calm down man. Please just calm down."

41

The words enter his mind with a convening clarity. He takes a deep breath. The noise dies down. He senses Robby and Jeff bulking up in the back. They're bigger than him. He couldn't take one of them, let alone two. Calm down, calm down. He sits perfectly still, takes another deep breath. They turn into his neighborhood. "It's this salmon colored one on the right." The driver pulls over. His expression stays the same.

"That'll be ten dollars."

In the back Robby and Jeff repeatedly jerk the door handles. "Why won't this door open?"

The passenger takes out his wallet and hands the driver a ten and two ones. "Appreciate the ride." He steps out of the car, walks to his door, takes his keys out of his pocket and inserts it into the lock. He can feel them leering at him. Inside his dog barks. He opens the door and shuts it behind him, locking it. His dog continues to growl. "It's just me," he says. "It's alright." The dog jumps onto the couch to peer out the blinds. Its ears are pulled back as it growls. It's a mutt, but it looks much like a fawn. He sits down on the couch and pulls the dog towards him. "It's okay, stop growling." He strokes its belly and takes a deep breath. "I'm not like that," he says. "I'm not like that."

Good Monday

They lower the seven thousand dollar casket down into the grave. It shines sharp of glazed mahogany. It was my brother's idea. "She deserves it," he said. Mother's corpse deserves it. My big brother Barry's brilliant idea. She deserves it, Mother deserves *Jesus Christ Mom. I can't believe they lock you up in this place. And you're paying good money for this dump*

It's okay Charlie.

When was the last time they dusted? It looks like a dust bunny shat his freaking pants in here. Are you sneezing? Are your sinuses bothering you at all?

I'm fine Charlie I promise.

And look at that TV. The color is so saturated, and the static buzz so loud. You pay good money for this place; they could at least give you a decent television.

It doesn't matter to me Charlie.

Well, I hate it. I hate everything about it, and I especially hate its name: hospice, like it's the changing of the name that kills you. I knew we shouldn't have picked this place, but Barry just wouldn't listen. You deserve better than this Ma

Oh please Charlie. My time here is only temporary. I'll be with your father soon and you won't have to worry but how can you be so sure? You don't know that how can you be so sure?

They start shoveling dirt into the grave and on top of the coffin. Dirt that the worms and the maggots will certainly piss and shit in. Piss and shit that will certainly ooze onto the seven thousand dollar, mahogany coffin that houses my mother's caramelized corpse. But there just ain't no sense in lettin' a perfectly fresh cadaver rot away is there, no sire! I want to be cremated when I die. I don't see any point in it whatsoever. Seven thousand dollars and you'll never see it again. To put a freeze-dried corpse into a seven thousand dollar box, and to then bury that box under six feet of dirt, is absurd.

Barry pounds the last bit of dirt onto the mound with round side of his shovel. My sister Lucille lays white lilies on top of the mound. She's crying. Barry wipes the sweat off his brow with his coat sleeve. His face looks red and puffy *I'm sorry Charlie but we decided it's best if I take over handling mother's assets and bank account. No Charlie look I told you Lucille and I both agreed that it was best it didn't matter if you agreed or not because we already decided by majority rule. It's only fair even if I would have consulted you beforehand and even if you said no beforehand we still would have beaten you two to one so I'm sorry Charlie it's only fair.* "Let's pray," he says. I watch my wife Angie and my two kids, Sarah and Bobby, bow their heads. Their noses sniffle in a synchronous pattern, like the crickets' sad eulogy.

We're cooking soup in the kitchen. I dice onions while Angie cuts carrots. There's an economical way to dice onions. You trim the ends off, slice it lengthwise into two hemispheres, lay a hemisphere flat on a surface, cut horizontally down the half, take a section, lay it down sideways, and carefully cut along the straight side. I find this method to be the most time efficient. Dicing onions forever is no way to live.

"Doesn't that upset your eyes?" asks Angie.

I slice.

"You know how much Mom left us when she died?" I say, "Six hundred and forty-four thousand dollars split between Barry and Lucille and me. Six hundred and forty-four thousand dollars."

"That's what you mother wanted, Charlie."

"Well, she made a misguided decision," I say. Angie looks up from the cutting board. Her eyebrows scrunch.

"What are you talking about, Charlie?"

"Look," I say, "All I'm saying is that by the time I'm dead I hope to have barely any money left."

"Oh really?" she says, "What about your legacy?"

"Hold on now Angie," I say, "Hold up. Let's make one thing clear. There's a big difference between a legacy and an inheritance. Legacy is poetic and a bunch of bullshit. Inheritance is just money that you didn't have enough time to spend. Don't conflate the two, please Angie. Besides, what kind of message do you think you're sending when you leave a lump sum of cash when you die?"

"I don't know, Charlie," she says, "maybe that you love and care about your children?"

"Oh, please Angie," I say, "They don't need it. They go to a good school, they make good grades, they'll get a good job and they'll make good money. They won't need that cash; they don't deserve it either. I swear Angie, when you get old and hold a pile of cash over their heads their going to push you right out the door Angie, I swear. You leave them a bunch of money and I'll tell you what your legacy will be. You'll be the one who worked too much and played too little, too stupid to spend your time wisely."

"Sure Charlie, but tell me this. What happens to me if you spend all of our money and die? What happens to me, Charlie?"

"Oh please Angie, don't be so melodramatic."

"Oh please you, Charlie," she says, "Your mother outlived your father by nearly fifteen years, but you don't think it could happen?"

"We can work something out."

"C'mon Charlie," she says, "You act like it's so important. It's just money. Let's talk about something else."

"Yeah, but don't be so naïve," I say, "Money is opportunity, Angie. Just think about it. We could go to Europe."

"You don't even like traveling," she says.

"But you've got a good point," I say, "Cause once you die, that money drops to zero value. That is if you're the dead body." Angie shrugs.

"Well," she says, "At least you won't need money in Heaven."

"But you don't know that!" I say, "How can you be so sure, you don't know that." The stairs creak. Angie's mouth hangs open.

"Please calm down Charles," she says, "My goodness what has gotten into you. And please put that knife down, you're swinging it around and it's scaring me." I take a deep breath.

"I'm sorry," I say, "I don't know what got into me." I scrape the diced onions off the cutting board and into a bowl.

I'm trying to cram the last piece of luggage into Sarah's car. I breathe deep and push hard into the suitcase to squeeze it into place, but it resists my urges. Sarah always says we should've gotten her an SUV, and I always say you should get less shit to fill fewer suitcases. That's what I think. I finally push it in, but I think I pulled my hamstring. Sarah walks out wearing a smile and a pair of sunglasses. "Thanks for helping me pack, Dad," she says.

"You're welcome, Sweetie," I say, "It was nice seeing you, even if the circumstances are less than preferable." She comes to embrace me with a hug.

"Oh, Dad," she says, "I'm so sorry. I'm so sorry about grandma."

"What do you have to be sorry about?" I say, "You didn't kill her." She looks up at me.

"Are you okay Dad?" she asks.

"I'm fine sweetie, really," I say, "don't worry about me I'm fine." She sniffles.

"Okay," she says, "I just can't help but worry about you sometimes."

"I promise I'm fine," I say, "You don't have to worry about me."

"Alright," she says. She lets go of me and wipes her face with her bare hands.

"Well," she says, "I guess I better get going."

"Alright," I say, "It was good seeing you."

"You too," she says, "Oh, hey Dad, do you have any cash? I need money for gas."

"Cash?" I say,

"Yeah," she says.

"Go ask your mother," I say. I walk away.

Charlie Banks

Charlie Banks, a young man wearing a white button down shirt and khakis that he bought at Walmart, walked into Huru, a meager sushi bar, with an earnest and melancholy expression. The time was 2:30 P.M. and besides a few lone customers and a Japanese woman standing at a desk in the front, the restaurant was empty. The Japanese woman, happy to see a customer, exclaims to Charlie in timid English, "Hello, welcome to Huru, how may I help you?" Charlie, in a mildly embarrassed manner responds, "Well ma'am, I'm gonna have to be honest with you, I do need help. You see hard times have fallen on me, and well, you can help me, I need a job." The woman, with a puzzled look on her face replies, "Here?"

"Why not?" responds Charlie, "Are y'all hiring?"

"I…I don't know,"

"Well, is the manager here?"

"No…not at the moment…isn't there somewhere else you can get a job?" inquired the woman.

"Yes ma'am I have, I've been just about everywhere, but I just haven't had any luck at all I guess," Charlie sighed, breaking eye contact. While scanning the room Charlie comes across peculiar porcelain statuette of a white cat raising its paw. With a tone of genuine curiosity, Charlie asks, "What's up with that cat?"

The woman, failing to understand why Charlie would ask that, and uneager to respond, says, "I…I don't know."

"Well is he waving or something like that, who's he waving to, customers or something?" asks Charlie.

"Um…I don't know…it's just decoration," the woman responds. An awkward silence ensues. Charlie spends a moment facing downward with his hands leaning against the desk, then, with a new spirit exclaims, "I'll tell you what, you don't have to promise me a job or nuthin', but you can at least let me fill out an application." The woman looked hesitant, but before she could respond, Charlie begged, "Please ma'am, out of the kindness of your heart." The woman, now desperate to alleviate the annoyance, gave in. "Okay," she said, "but I need to go to the back office to print one."

"That's fine, go ahead," said Charlie.

The woman slowly walked to the back shaking her head in confusion, and as soon as she crossed through the door, Charlie, now sporting a sly grin, picked up the porcelain cat and left.

Character Sketch essay for Ben's freshman writing class at the University of Mississippi, courtesy of Tyler Ricketts.

Whirlpool in Winter

Winter coats the whirlpool trails—
snow stuck cedar, pine and birch.
Strange striations on the gravel
like the fossil of a fish
ancient and colossal,
or the spectral tracks of a railroad past—
still secrets to unravel.

Turn onto a solitary trail—
the disembodied highway wails—
and all along the forest floor are
spider webs dusted with snow—
the silken traps exposed.

A helicopter shears the frigid air—
thick fog skims the surface
of muddy water
the color of milk and coffee—
pink plastic ribbons tied to trees,
bent northward—
the powerlines point to
the daylight moon, from night
to morning purchase.

If I recommended a book to Ben, he was quick to read it and eager to discuss. I always enjoyed his take and often he would have insights that I missed. Now, if he enjoyed the book or found it particularly interesting he would return the favor and recommend a book to me. And I, in turn, would read what he recommended. I *always* benefited from his recommendations. Ben truly had an incredible mind. He could draw on disparate pieces of knowledge and tie them together into a cohesive idea. When he was in a good place, it was a joy to watch his brain work.

- From Ben's therapist and friend, Baxter Hogue

Part Two

Contributed Writings

by Ben's Friends

God's Love

By Michael Gray

My name is Michael Gray and I would like to reflect the moments I shared with Ben. As my mind look back not even a year ago, I think of my friend and I met on my job at Millbrook Cricket Farm. At Millbrook, we raise and sell crickets all over the United States. When Ben was hired, I had just changed positions which made us directly interacting to complete the goals of the company. I must admit my personality being more introverted than extroverted, I was settled that getting to know Ben would be hard. My previous position at Millbrook I was alone with my work, this was a big change for me.

The reason I say this is because I have never had to interact on a daily basis with someone of a different ethnic group. With so much of the past still being part of our future, it is difficult to won't to get to know, or trust, someone outside the ones you call your family.

Being a born again Christian doesn't make me perfect. Romans 3:10 says; As it is so naturally my mind would wonder if Ben had already characterized me by the color of my skin. Boy was I in for a good surprise. One morning on my way to work I stopped by a favorite donut shop to get breakfast. As I ordered my food, I got a notion to get some extra to share with someone. The someone I thought I was going to share with was not going there that morning. When I begin to eat my pastry with my coffee, I offered Ben some, and to my surprise he accepted. This started the friendship between Ben and I.

The act of Ben expecting what I hope to offer opened the door to us getting to know each other better. This really made me feel comfortable to know that he believed that I would do him no harm. We begin to share not only food but also ideas and beliefs. The way we begin to interact with each other you would have think we been friends since childhood. I could go on and on about the different scenarios and fun times we experienced at Millbrook but either I will run out of paper or my hand will fall off from writing.

Even though Ben and I come from a different background we shared a familiar spirit. The familiar spirit was not our personalities, it was the love of Jesus Christ. Our minds are quick to prejudge a person especially someone from a different culture or background. But if the Love of God abide in our heart, we will give that person a chance to prove themselves.

Ben gave me a chance and I proved myself as a good person to him. I gave Ben a chance and he proved himself good to me. I hope this friendship between Ben and I enlighten those who needed to hear this. This is a perfect example of God's Love. The Love of God has no color barrier. No matter if you are green, purple, God Loves you the same as he loves you the same as he loves me. If we would all share the same love, which is the love of Jesus Christ this world would be able to start it's healing from the past and then only this country can really become great again!

To my friends who have passed
By Sam Kealhofer

We're just left gussin'
At some of life's biggest questions
And all we get's
An empty sky
When we're looking out for heaven.

And the moon with its crescent
Sings the song of our own evanescence.

For we are ethereal beings,
Simply angles with snipped wings.
Forced to trudge through the
Mud, shit, and piss
Of everyday experience

To earn that eternal time
Spent basking
In an everlasting sunshine

The memories of our friends.

Southern Gothic

By Sam Kealhofer

Well Daddy didn't teach me much
Except to not fall for the same trick twice,
And Mamma used to always say
The good Lord don't roll no dice.

I suppose that means
He's not a gambling man,
But I'm not quite sure
Of how that pertains
Cause what's the big man got to gain?

Well Daddy didn't teach me much
Expect how to play a mean round of pool,
And how to eye the crowd
To tell a player from a fool.

Daddy liked to play the odds.
Would put a Jackson and a Jameson
Atop the pool table,
And butter up some poor sap
With words as sweet as maple.

After Daddy would win
He'd throw back the Jameson,
And ask if they'd want to rack again.
Either way, He'd order another whiskey on ice,
And the whole time I'd just think
Of how the good Lord don't roll no dice.

I guess that means
Daddy's not much of a godly man,
And I'd often wonder
How that fit into the Lord's plan.

Well once I told Momma
I didn't much comprehend
How come God made us this way
And still punish us for sin?
She just shook her head,
Stared at me a moment, and said
Boy, the devil does what you ask of him
But that don't make him a friend.

Burning Down the House

By Reid Haynie

It was cold, early February, humidity lingering from summer and biting deep in my chest. I sat close to the heat tower under the overhang. A jeep pulled up—a mid 2000s Cherokee, *Born Under Punches* blasting from the radio disturbing the quiet night shut off, and the figure emerged from the driver-side door. He wore an olive green military jacket, light against the biting, wet cold, and dabbed out his Camel Blue cigarette. Red, thinning hair. Skin fair like butter. I finished a Budweiser, Alex ate pork tacos, we sat on the porch of the Jackson, Mississippi barbeque joint.

"What's up guys," Ben said, shivering in his hand-me-down army coat. "Thanks for making it out."

"Hey, man," I said. "You nervous?"

"Nah, it'll be fine."

He was nervous. It was evident before he arrived, evident by his insistence that we come out and sit in the cold. It was Tuesday night Trivia at The Pig & Pint. Drew Brunson would arrive there shortly, and so would Topher, all of us to support Ben on his first night of hosting trivia, all of us to bury him five months later on a 102 degree Mississippi Saturday, Summer 2017.

In Oxford I sat on my futon, *Born Under Punches* blasting from the bathroom accompanying one of Ben's drawn-out showers. I was reading a draft of his thesis short story collection, *Dreams About Food*. Tyler was on campus grading freshman geology labs. Ben's dog Charlotte lay next to me on the futon. I loved that dog. From the far side of the wall the song changed. Ben's stories were funny. He had a knack for it, for making you laugh til your chest ached like February cold. I read about finagling waiters, alien abduction, eating blueberry toaster strudels stoned off your ass. He work-shopped standup routines to me on that same futon. *In order to be elected president, you have to suck at least five dicks*, he once told me, emotive, pacing my bedroom as I sat cleaning blown glass with isopropyl. *That's how you know Donald Trump is going to win. Donald Trump's sucked so many dicks, Hillary doesn't have a chance. She wouldn't even suck Bill's dick. He had to have an intern for that.*

I told Ben he should take his futon five public, but he was too aware of a stage, of a microphone before a silent room. Along the line though he decided that hosting trivia was the perfect bridge. That reading prompts weekly behind a folding table would force it all into his comfort zone, that he could learn to work a crowd into laughter as he so easily managed in more organic settings.

"I'm going to go let them know I'm here."

Ben walked to the hosting table under the overhang. I could see his nervousness as he stepped. He greeted the host, his trainer. Drew arrived with his brother Tommy, joining the rest of us at the long, splintery table. I switched to PBR.

Trivia host training works like this: the first half, you observe. Each round features a question, followed by an approximately three minute song, allotting the time for submitting answers. Half-time comes around, five minutes of music as progress is tallied. Then, the second half, you the trainee take over, your handler close by to keep you on the rails.

During the first half Ben nervously waited, flirting with his friends with his eyes, ignoring his inevitable emergence to the forefront of everyone's trivial experience. Half time, Ben increasingly stirred. Progress was tallied. We were eleventh out of fourteen teams. Ben stirring, music playing. Cheap PA speakers and cold biting wind.

"For the second half I'm going to hand it over to Ben Ingram who is training with us tonight, so give him a warm welcome as he hosts his very first trivia." The mic patted loudly changing hands, then total silence.

"Yes... ehm."

I came home from class, and Charlotte greeted me inside the front door. Through the living room I saw the backdoor standing open, and I walked through the house with Charlotte waging beside me to find Ben in the backyard. He paced anxiously, smoking a cigarette. 2015 had turned into 2016, the year of our graduation, and it was at this point when we began to realize how unprepared we were for whatever came next.

"How'd the Coates quiz go?"

"Fine, I finished reading it this morning. It was pretty good."

"Yeah I thought you'd like it." He finished off a camel blue, dropping it into the coffee pot next to the door.

Charlotte panted, still excited to see me. I chased her around the yard through the track she had dug with months of running the backyard fence. I could no longer smell the accumulating butts by the door as Charlotte and I made our way behind the hydrangea bushes, which were blooming in the early March heat. Ben was quiet on the porch. Fretting, losing hair, focusing on something so internal I could only sense it in his pacing the porch beams.

That year he had grown more and more preoccupied. He had quit reading, quit writing. He said he no longer had the concentration for it. His piles of books were just piles. In his room, on his desk, on the living room floor. Piles of untapped inspiration. The kitchen piled with dirty dishes. Wendy's bags, empty bottles of Dark Horse Cabernet. Piles of mounting irresponsibility. He told me about sleepless nights and paralyzing dreams. Of no appetite all day and binge-eating late at night. I had begun to notice a tremor in his eyelids whenever he sat down. Frantic, violent, eyes rolled back with their lids flashing open and closed as if possessed by some terrible thing. He said it had started when he quit his medication. It did not subside when he got back on it.

We went upstairs in pursuit of a/c. Ben sat on the futon, his eyes immediately rolling back, lids flickering as I watched from the end of my bed. We sat there silently, his arms folded over the top of his head, and I hooked my phone up to the stereo. I watched him sitting, eyes flickering, he faced upward, seeming to battle himself within, and it came out through his stiffening arms and toes. I sat at an impossible distance from him. Ben was in a world only his. He told me what it was like on the inside, but I could never come in. That was out of his control. I watched between worlds at the violence within his eye sockets and in his rigid feet. Then, the chorus.

Slowly, panic begin to subside, and he started to mouth along. His arms relaxed a little. The expanse between us dissolving before my eyes. His pupils rolled forward, and his toes lost their rigidity from beneath his dog-haired socks. I watched his mouth moving with the words, emitting a barely audible signal. He animated more, sang louder, became insincere and playful like we always knew him. Charlotte rose on her front legs. Her tongue lapped, and Ben was five years younger laughing about Goonch catfish and pranking his way out of a job at the Malco Grandview. He was rearranging Santa boxes to spell Satan and making fun of my hairy feet. He sat upright on the futon and raised his arms anthemic-like toward the ceiling now belting out the words. Such moments of reversal said that whatever he was struggling with wasn't as permanent as he insisted it was, that it was only youthful and temporary, that deep down he was the same funny, irreverent bastard we knew he was.

We managed to graduate that semester. Ben finished his thesis right under the wire. After seven or so months he and I were both back in Jackson, losing time to HBO and inebriation, and he finally found the motivation to pursue his dream of stand-up comic by way of trivia night host.

"New York-born pop star known as the 'Songbird Supreme' began her acting career with the 2001 box office success 'Glitter'. Who is this singer slash actress Mariah Carey – oh god dammit."

Ben dropped the mic to the folding table and turned to his trainer. Saying the answer at the end of a prompt is generally unacceptable in hosting trivia. The crowd murmured quietly. I nervously sipped beer as Ben's complexion turned from egg-white to red-bean. The trainer scrolled to find a replacement question. "Sorry guys. It'll just be one second," Ben added into the microphone, returning it to the table.

That night Drew and I stayed over. Ben shuffled on the back porch fighting the cold through his thin coat.

"They're going to have me at Lost Pizza every Tuesday starting next week." He lit a cigarette excitedly. Drew brought us beer from inside, leaving the extra three in their plastic rings by the back door.

"Where is that, exactly?"

"It's over there in Maywood Mart. I can't remember what used to be there." He played a song through the Bluetooth speaker.

Drew and I sat cold against the wall as Ben paced the yard excitedly. He was forgetful of the hangups, of the Mariah Careys. "It pays like a hundred bucks a night," he said enthusiastically. "It's like an actual job!"

Charlotte walked alongside Ben down the Natchez trace walking trail. She matched him step for step despite the midday heat, despite the four or so miles they'd already covered.

Sleepless nights, no appetite and lots and lots of coffee. Up nineteen hours a day and Charlotte lay quietly next to us on the couch. *Don't call me with anything that you can just tell me in person.*

I think the FBI has my phone tapped. Yours too, probably. "MUSIC." He said. "No, no," the trainer interjected. "*Play* music. Don't *say* 'music'. You have to play music to start the round."

Ben sat in the total darkness of the living room, but I could still see his eyes which were softly illuminated by the window light, and they flickered like hell, trapping him there inside them.

Don't cross me, motherfucker. Who the hell cares what I smell like?

I love you guys. *Don't fucking cross me.*

You know who else smelled bad? Jesus, probably.

Drew took another beer from the six pack rings. He handed it to me. "Yeah, man. We'll come," he said. "I like trivia. Now we have something to do on Tuesdays." I said, "same" and took the beer. Ben talked about New York City.

Jackson is a place to grow restless. I set my eyes on the next stage of things and decided the next stage was in Austin, Texas. My last night in town I got "JXN" tattooed on my calf and then played a show in Midtown with The Vagrant Family Band. Ben and Drew came. At the end of the show I was saying goodbye to all of my Jackson friends. "I hope the best for you, I really do," Ben told me as I was loading gear into my car. The sincerity struck me. It was unusual.

I drove out of Jackson listening to Talking Heads. I drove thinking about Ben, hopefully. I didn't know that trivia was his last stand, that reading deadpan from an Excel document for eight or ten people a week was the last push to make something stick, his writing, his comedy, his big-moment plans to move to New York City boiled down to that final weekly assault behind a Costco folding table. I didn't know that his goodbye the night before was really a goodbye. I turned up the radio, driving west with the morning sun behind me. I drove away feeling I did my part. That Ben would bounce back strong as ever. The knowledge of the past to guide him on. Sixty days and counting to a 102 degree Mississippi Saturday, Summer 2017.

Fire

By Finn Udall

I.

These flames lick like you licking
the place on my chest
where scarecrows stand above waving hair
quiet, still, staring

my skin is wet with your spit
shimmering, steaming in the heat
of a patch of ground burning,
the flames flicking high into the air
above my head, searing my hair

I step into the patch of fire

inside the fire, I mingle with the androgynous ghosts
of people who left their homes
like I left my home
and who lived in their own loud chaoses
of heroin binges and bad trips
like I lived on a racetrack
speeding and pacing around powder-covered coffee tables

ghosts who were abused by their fathers
because they were small
and pretty and alive, and abused by their boyfriends
or whoever happened to be around,
ghosts who were pushed down or pushed away

or pulled through a strainer because they were found
doing the wrong thing with the wrong person
in the wrong public restroom

ghosts who lived in streets,
gutters dirty with broken needles,
and slept in tents in gray courtyards
in the middles of their cities, pushing grocery carts
in the rain over chipped cobblestones
or cracked sidewalks, overgrown with weeds

in three years
we're all lighting off bottlerockets
down by the river,
and if you look closely
you can see your image reflected,
distorted in the water
but there's something else there

something behind you

II.

perfection is black space

my dad has broken his nose twelve times,
his chin is crooked,
and he has skin cancer from old sunburns

when I'm walking barefoot on the sidewalk in the summer
and the concrete burns my feet,
I think of him in the boxing ring
and how exciting the feeling of a glove in his face
must have been

how exciting it is for me

they kicked me out

I took a greyhound to Portland
and this is what Portland is:
A man dressed all in pink
let out the Doors from a fuzzy boom box
and danced on the courtyard benches
while we smoked his weed
and played folk punk songs on used guitars
with our hats upturned on the ground

in the hospital waiting room,
I am the melting remains
of a burning candle
fighting against the fluorescent lights
to find a seat on this crowded bus

my dad says, "when you ran away,
it was a pretty big fuck-you to us, but this,
this is the biggest fuck-you of all"
and he looks like the tip of an arrow,
trying to get lodged in something

They pump me full of saline and activated charcoal
and all those pills
come flowing out in a black sludge
from my mouth

My mom tried to wash off
what I wrote in sharpie
on the concrete next to my bed
but the soap wasn't strong enough,
and I know how the soap feels

every night when I come home from college
I light a match to read

the little black letters
on the concrete next to my bed

The light isn't bright enough
to wake my little brother,
seventeen and sleeping in my old bed

I read those words and remember them
coming into me through headphones,
one hundred aspirin tabs dissolved in a glass of water,
sweating into the loving arms of black sheets,
ears ringing, heart blinking, teeth stinging

"I'm going to kill everybody in this room"

III.

Stepping into the flames
is coming to a new country
where you only have a vague understanding
of the language

I put the fire into my mouth,
popped like time release capsules
that empty out and dissolve into my blood,
make it hot

my body is a tree with a flame
burning in the hollow trunk

my body is a knife
stuck in the sharpener
You're the sun and I'm the moon
and together, we're the turning omnipresent eyes
of a great head, the great body of foamy galaxies
that twists around my finger

pointing upward, at a punk show on a shaky arm

the hands of the clock twitch,
push into my veins
and I'm always worried I didn't clean them
well enough as they turn inside me,
little hot points blossoming with moments
of inertia, the deep, wasted places
that I keep in my small cages

my vision is filled with colors
blinking in and out
like the sun trying to hide
behind the turning blades of a windmill

so many suicides end up
under microscopes, the biology
of abandonment contained in a heavy leather-bound book

the second hand is a slow, single
turning blade that comes down to
cut me in half, but what can I do
besides sit down and wait?

Sometimes I think that I walked through the fire
and am better for it, but then in the morning
I look in the mirror
and I see that my skin is still pure and milky
and covered in flames

Whisping Tide

By William Moore

There's a sort of path—a trackline,
where pale yellow sneakers blended sand and mud,
perforating the beach with size 7 holes
which dissolve with morning's tide
stretching to the pines.

I've walked here before,
but my footprints never linger,
yanked in by mud-sand
enriched with beer cans and twigs.
I try matching my strides with
the size 7s, but I fall to my bruises,
unable to keep the perfect timing
between pale yellow steps.

The wind roars in one ear,
then trickles across my face and whispers
into the other. The pale steps are fading,
but I can't stop following them
until my own steps gurgle
with the inward tide,
and I take shelter behind the pines.

Warmth

By William Moore

A person of grace, willing to take the fall
For my childish mistakes, committed often
In weakness, unable to give my all
At times I laugh with you side-saddled
And dream of what's to come for us,
Refreshed, crisp like sun-baked leaves
But I fear the hidden, unable to know
where I'll next be collar-dragged
In circles, ineptly drawn through the muck
And yet again, your warmth finds me,
nurses me, and drives away the head-fog
that brushed away my progress like a fir branch
dragged behind a snow path
I lost your redemptive embrace
Your tender arms entwined and clutching,
Sweet breath hazing my shoulder with damp love
Water me with your heart -
My dried hope is a pallor-wrought creekbed,
But you slake the thirst of rivers.

Pig Heart

By Rachel Vise

hooved feet pound into skull stampede down
Cheeks built of dead father's bone
I smell this giant's blood in the
sour green rivers that weave
through marrow peeling
thick like wallpaper
thin like ham
dripping damp stench down
back my soft skull
gouge out red eyes weeping
menstrual blood minstrel mud
song of mangled limbs
shouting daddy's jowls immortal
child wailing like a doe
jaw shot clean off
soft piss stained feeble shit dripping
rubies down hog thigh
squeal little girl
little lamb moaning
groaning dig my grave
crawl down sobbing nocturne number
six feet under beaming worms
moonlit yodel screams sonata
not fourteen—*fifteen*
fourteen crooning fifteen dead
fifteen minutes noiseless shrieking and
fifteen numb white buck meat dread
while he hangs like a picture

belt buckle broken
esophagus crushed c-minor sharp
solemn chanting dead man swaying
did you hear my daddy howl

The Night at the Landfill

By Tyler Ricketts

It was a weekend and Ben and I were at his house. We were having a good time talking and doing our normal weekend rituals together that we found comfort in. Fast food, movies, tasteful jokes, talks about Radiohead and The Gorillaz, and just about anything else that would come to our minds.

During our weekend we had received a text that there was a party that night and all of our friends were there. We both debated about going or not. We were both content shooting the shit at home and taking it easy, it was comfortable, and the thought of putting shoes on was like committing a crime. We thought about what we were going to do and could not make up our minds. We knew we should be social, but we were indifferent about going.

Ben said that we should at least show our face at the party. A quick entrance, a few hellos and goodbyes and then return to our relaxing weekend. I agreed, but I asked about how the hell were we going to go about this? We both knew when going to a party with all of our friends they would want to talk and talk and want to hangout. So after thinking of our game plan of being in and out, Ben proposed an idea that was so brilliantly funny that I couldn't say no.

"Does your dad still work for the garbage company?" he said.

"Yeah," I responded. Why does that matter though?"

"Wouldn't it be funny if we pretended like we just got jobs at the landfill so we had to wake up at like 5 a.m. to go to work? It would be the perfect plan to leave the party early!" Ben replied.

I bursted out laughing. "This could totally work, but how are people going to believe us?" I asked.

"Dude. We need to go to Walmart and find some jumpsuits and wear them to the party. Then we'll look like we work there."

"Brilliant!"

We went to Walmart, got jumpsuits, and put them on and headed to the party. Everyone was glad to see us and kept asking what's with the jumpsuits? We kept s straight face and said something along the lines of "Yeah, we got jobs at the landfill a few weeks ago and have to go into work around 5. Probably won't be able to stay long but hey good to see you!"

The funny part was that everyone was some level of drunk and they believed us. The plan worked! Some people even asked us for jobs for summer work! So we ended up being there for about an hour and then both gave the signal that it was time to dip. We left and got in the car quietly and then looked at each other. I can't remember who burst out laughing first but it was like a chain reaction and we laughed the entire way home talking about all the silly conversations we had. From that day on we both kept those jumpsuits for safe keeping, as a memento to remember the perfect plan, the perfect weekend night. It's been about 7 years and I still wear that damn thing and laugh.

Angel

By Michael Tusa

It's so uncomfortable
being an Angel in a sack

no place for your wings
and your halo always drooping down
as you try to light your cigarette . . .

your tunic always getting dirtied up
and always catching on loose nails
and splinters and always being torn
by all of the unkind foreign objects
who could never truly appreciate something so soft.

so many times, I watched you
fly around the kitchen
beer in hand
casting your chuckle
onto each and every wall
and laughing at the words
as we watched them spill out on the table

The reflection of our lives loved living in your grin

Did you give it all away?
Or lose it somewhere on the journey
between the stars and your bed?

Something about reaching for the secret
too soon

seems appropriate

Something about how this is all
just a big misunderstanding

and how the wheels roll
around and around
and around

and that the play is not over
and this is just an interlude
an intermission
a pause
and you are awaiting us
behind the curtain
ready to deliver the punch line
to the ultimate joke

Afterword

The Benson Reed Ingram Scholarship

The Benson Reed Ingram Scholarship

On July 22nd, 2017, after battling anxiety and depression for many years, my twin brother Ben took his own life. Ben found solace from inner demons in his pursuit to become a writer. While at the University of Mississippi, his quest culminated in his senior honor's thesis: a brilliant collection of fictional short stories he titled *Dreams About Food.*

On July 22nd, 2018, on the anniversary of Ben's suicide, our family formed the Benson Reed Ingram Scholarship Fund at the University of Mississippi. The fund awards those who, like Ben, courageously apply to the join the Honor's college in their junior year. Upon endowment, one or more annual awards will be made in Ben's name, and his legacy will live on at Ole Miss—forever.

Our family appreciates any support of Ben's scholarship fund, no matter how small. You can donate online at **DreamsAboutFood.com.** While you're there, be sure to grab a Dreams About Food T-Shirt, coffee mug, or an extra copy of the book. Since you're a reader of this book, be sure to use promo code "DREAMS" at checkout and you'll receive a free coffee mug on orders over $30 (Ben *loved* coffee.)

Prefer to donate by check, instead?

Mail a check made payable to *The Benson Reed Ingram Scholarship Fund* with Acct #06196 in the memo. Mailing address below:
> University of Mississippi Foundation
> Memory House
> 406 University Avenue
> Oxford, MS 38655

Thank you so much for reading *Dreams About Food.* If you have feedback, please feel free to email me at lee.dreamsaboutfood@gmail.com.
With Love,
Lee Ingram